I0533821

AutoCEO

Sarah Neofield

*"What did you do in your job as
CEO today?"
"Nothing."*

This book is dedicated to the best CEO I know, Oliver
S., and to Lydia S., for keeping him honest.

And, of course, to my favourite cyborg, Zoë M. May
you continue to become harder, better, faster, stronger.

Copyright © 2022 Sarah Neofield

All rights reserved.

ISBN: 978-1-922362-06-3

PART 1

CHAPTER 1

It had to be at least an inch bigger. Thicker, that was. With gold lettering. And twice as many color inserts.

Replacing Noel Skum's biography on its shelf, Hugh returned to the mess of photos spread across his desk.

Gathering pictures to fill the glossy color pages of his autobiography was about the only real work he'd done for the book.

Originally, Hugh was supposed to be writing a volume on leadership and management. His trademark 'hands-off' approach.

The sort of book that shot to the top of the bestseller charts (with a few thousand strategically placed sales at key bookshops, orchestrated by a team of paid buyers).

The sort of book that got plastered across the backs of buses, and talked about reverentially in business schools, with learned professionals reading his words aloud to an audience.

Hugh had put a lot of thought into getting his business philosophy down on paper. Know yourself. Honesty is the best policy. Be your own brand. You can't please everyone.

He'd written down all his original thoughts, all his witty sayings. But his editor said that none of them were exactly original. 'Cliches', she'd said. What garbage.

There were more: Dare to dream. Call people by name. Take every opportunity. Learn to say 'no'. Manifest your destiny.

That last one, Hugh admitted, made him sound a bit too much like some hippy-dippy new-age guru. Though, when his editor had pressed him to explain the success he enjoyed – in spite of his abysmal grades, lack of real-world experience, and the string of sexual harassment claims against him - 'I manifested my destiny' was the best Hugh could come up with.

After eighteen months of fruitless meetings and missed deadlines, Hugh's editor had gently suggested he try his hand at an autobiography instead, mumbling something about a 'small down payment' to cover the ghostwriting and printing expenses, which Hugh thought was a funny way to describe what he could only imagine would be a six-figure advance.

In a sense, Hugh was relieved. Truth be told, he hadn't done enough actual leading to fill up a page, let alone an entire book on management.

What Hugh really wanted, of course, was one of those books with "Unauthorized biography of..." on the cover.

'Why would you want that?' his agent had asked when he first suggested printing it on the front.

Hugh could hardly tell her the real reason.

He wanted one of those biographies that began with the writer describing how doggedly they'd pursued him. How many times they'd begged him to share his story before he finally, gracefully acquiesced – probably at an upscale seafood restaurant with a harbor view. He wanted to be chased. To play hard to get.

Paying someone to ghostwrite your autobiography because you couldn't even write about your own life in a way others found authentic, let alone interesting, was shameful. But having someone write about your life without your permission? To probe every little detail of your personal life, noting every idiosyncrasy of taste, every deviancy? That was flattering.

Now, as he sat chewing – or attempting to chew – the end of one of his thick, engraved pens, Hugh was beginning to suspect he hadn't lived enough to fill an entire book, either. At least, not if you were going to cut out all the bits that made him seem 'unrelatable', 'selfish' or – what was the other thing Maddy had said? 'Spoilt.'

Without enough achievements to crow about, Maddy, the ghostwriter Hugh had been assigned, had suggested he pad the book out with glowing endorsements from his rich and powerful friends.

So far, he'd amassed six pages of salivating nonsense – seven, if the publisher agreed to use the font size Hugh always used for his annual reports in the years the company's achievements were similarly thin. The size – 12.3 points – was just large enough to boost the page count, but to the untrained eye, the difference was imperceptible. A trick Hugh had perfected back in his school days.

It served him well, at least until St Lucre's started requiring electronic submission of essays, and the teachers wised up to his low word count. Hugh had been mistrustful of computers ever since.

Hugh's story wasn't especially inspiring to what Maddy called 'real people'. 'Real people,' she'd said 'can't relate to a CEO whose job was handed to them because their father was friends with the guy who used to run the company.'

Nor was his life story particularly admirable. Hugh had neither overcome any particular adversity, nor achieved anything extraordinary. Unless you counted having amassed the country's largest collection of belt buckles. Or winning CEO Magazine's Best Dressed Manager of a B&S 500 Company. Of course, that was back when his wife had insisted he hire a personal stylist. Ex-wife, Hugh corrected himself.

At any rate, you needed one of those two things to sell a book. Guts or glory. And, in spite of Maddy's best efforts to extract something resembling either a human or a superhuman side from him, Hugh had neither to offer.

Still, he had heard that writing could be a reflective process, and indeed, writing the book – or having the book written for him – was making Hugh reassess his life.

Important men, Hugh knew, had mistresses. Finding one had been at the top of his to-do list for years. Although, technically, he realized, any female companion he did manage to find would be a girlfriend rather than a mistress, now that his second divorce had been finalized. If he wanted to find a mistress, Hugh needed to find another wife first. Preferably one that didn't call him an 'emotionless robot'.

His former assistant Alyssa, at a stretch, might have been a suitable candidate for the mistress category, but she was a long way short of wife material.

For a time, Hugh had cultivated a variety of little habits that set him apart from his peers specifically in the hopes that they would one day provide some simpering young writer in a short skirt with ample fodder to pen a glowing account of his quirky eccentricities.

He'd even taken to wearing black shirts and jeans for a while, tossing out all of his suits in the hopes of cultivating a recognizable 'look'. That had only lasted for the three days Bambi was out of town. As soon as she returned, the t-shirts were in the trash, and Hugh had his first appointment with Ken the 'personal stylist'. 'If you want to make a statement,' Bambi had said, 'at least let a professional tell you what to wear.'

She had a point, really. After all, he'd only started wearing the black shirts after Dan mentioned in an interview that he wore the same thing each day because it reduced the number of unimportant choices he had to make each day, freeing his brain cells for more important choices. Of course, as Bambi had pointed out, the most important decision Hugh made each day was what to have for lunch.

For a time, Hugh had taken to eating at McKing's every time the company made a new acquisition, even though he could afford far better, and the company undertook so many takeovers and mergers that the tradition had fallen by the wayside. Hugh's digestive system couldn't handle the rapidity with which the company swallowed up other companies.

Besides, Bambi was right. Nobody at the company ever sought his opinion on anything, save for his assistant asking what he wanted for lunch. Hugh could easily while away several hours of a morning pondering menus – on the days he came into the office. Without that task, he was lost. In fact, he felt as if he wasn't contributing at all.

What was the point of cultivating a distinctive personality if nobody was clamoring to write an unauthorized biography about him? If he was going to have to pay someone to do it?

Writing a life story was a lot like sex, Hugh thought. He much preferred his partner to comply out of admiration rather than in exchange for cash. In fact, the analogy gaining traction in his mind, it was *exactly* the same. You couldn't brag about having your life immortalized by a ghostwriter any more than you could brag about bedding a prostitute. Although, on reflection, Hugh realized, several of his friends did. Maybe, he gulped, hiring a ghostwriter was worse. After all, the whole idea of a ghostwriter was their invisibility.

Ostensibly, it was Hugh writing the book – not Maddy. Even though in reality, he had written just as much of his "autobiography" as he had written of his chairman's letters over the last decade, which was to say not a word. It was all well and good to have some dewy-eyed sycophant write rapturously about your eccentric sense of style or charming little rituals. But if Hugh was seen to be exposing these details about himself – well, he'd just look like a lunatic.

No, the best thing to do was adopt the strategy he'd so often relied upon throughout the years – to lie low, say little other than carefully crafted, empty platitudes, rely on the endorsements of his friends, and turn up at the book launch wearing whatever suit his stylist recommended, to sign his name on yet another stack of pages he'd never read.

'Your meeting with Madison Presley begins in five minutes,' Myra announced. Ever since Alyssa's departure, he'd relied on a digital assistant to keep his appointments with Madison – or Maddy, as Hugh called her, even though she pulled a face every time he did. Madison was a man's name, if ever he'd heard one.

When his editor assigned Hugh a ghostwriter, explaining the book would still be marketed as an 'auto' biography even if he wasn't the one actually putting pen to paper, Hugh had imagined some cute young thing in a mini-skirt who'd hang off his every word.

Usually, Hugh had no issue taking credit for the work of others. But this time, he'd been quite excited about the prospect of one of those biographies where a smitten author would write, in rapturous detail, how his mind worked like a sophisticated machine. A computer that processes input, replicating it in his mind's eye as though his brain were equipped with a graphics chip, allowing him to process the algorithmic interrelations of the numbers and figures he encountered. That's how he'd put it to Maddy. Although he wasn't quite sure what an algorithm was. Or whether a graphics chip was the right… thing. But it was the only part of a computer Hugh had heard of, primarily because his teenage son went on about them.

Writing that sort of thing about yourself would sound conceited. Even Hugh knew that. It was a different matter if a biographer quoted you as explaining that your brain worked like a computer, as opposed to the nauseating soft tissue all those inadequate to rise to the rank of CEO possessed. A skilled writer, he knew, could couch such a quote in enough admiration to make Hugh's assessment of himself sound almost humble. Hell, after witnessing some of the stunning manipulations he'd seen in the chairman's letters he'd had his writers massage over the years, Hugh believed that writers could do anything.

The short-haired woman with a bit of a tummy taking a seat in one of the chairs he'd had specially lowered was precisely the opposite of who Hugh had expected. Still, Maddy was only the second most unattractive woman he'd had the misfortune to meet over the previous year.

The worst, by far, was that awful woman from the union, Lila, who had even shorter hair, and an even more lumpy rear. Her personality was equally unappealing. She was always bringing up phrases like 'illegal working conditions' and 'unfair dismissal' - as if there could be such a thing! Hugh had never heard anything more ludicrous in his life. The company had a right – nay, a duty – to terminate anyone it liked. 'Fairness' didn't even begin to factor into the equation.

If he'd had a half-decent assistant, Lila would have never made it into the building, let alone to his floor, or through his office door. Permitting Lila to come and harass him was why he'd had to let Alyssa go. The fact that her firing coincided with her filing a complaint against him was nothing more than coincidence.

Hugh shuddered. Lila had given him enough trouble this past year with her unreasonable demands. Campaigning for an end to monitored toilet breaks. For the introduction of sick leave. Almost preventing the rollout of the AutoAutomator. The sort of crap that left him – and CGM – exposed to frivolous lawsuits filed by some bozo that disgruntled workers found advertised on a bus seat on their way to work. Or worse, a class action suit on behalf of all those losers who couldn't pay for their own representation.

'Let's get down to business, Mr. Richardson. I know you're a very busy man,' Maddy said. 'Tell me about your childhood.'

Hugh had been preparing for this question, but it still made him feel as if he were on his therapist's couch, instead of sitting bolt upright in his own chair, at his own desk, in his own office. It was an altogether unfamiliar setting.

He checked his watch – the Triple Diamond Platinum Hubris Excalibur Pete'd had the gall to point out was 'so two years ago'. His words still stung. Pete, of course, was one of those men with a luxury watch subscription, in large part due to a competition with his one-time co-CEO. Each month, a new one was automatically delivered to his house in a polished wood case. It was a business expense, Pete explained. The watch subscription allowed him to keep his finger on the pulse, so to speak, without having to waste time doing research and shopping.

Three o'clock. Normally, Hugh would be playing golf at this hour.

Taking a breath, Hugh launched into his well-rehearsed family history. The story of how, with only a small loan from his great-great-grandfather, his great-grandfather had started the company which Hugh's grandfather, and then his father, and then Hugh himself had run. Right up until it was de-listed.

He was about to explain how, really, the company going under was in the best interest of the investors and employees, and how he himself had used his $13 million payout to buy a holiday home – the one his ex-wife had tried to claim – before he nabbed the top job at CGM, when Maddy interrupted.

'Any youthful pranks? We need something funny, or heartwarming. Something that will endear you to the reader.'

Hugh had just the thing.

'You could write about the time I got suspended!'

Maddy's pen paused mid-air. A cheap plastic thing, like the ones Alyssa used to use. 'That sounds promising. What happened?'

Hugh shuffled through the photos on his desk until he found the right one.

'Pete and I, and a bunch of the other guys from St Lucre's, cut ethics class one afternoon, just before summer vacation, to drive down to the beach in my dad's Luxxari.'

'And you were suspended?' Maddy frowned at the photograph. But it was an impressed frown, Hugh could tell. He was used to women pulling faces that appeared to be expressions of derision or concern, but which, he knew, were actually expressions of deep admiration – with perhaps, even, a touch of lust. 'For how long?'

'Well, the suspension lasted less than half an hour. As soon as my father arrived, it was all sorted out.'

'And what did your dad say?'

Hugh chuckled. 'He gave me the Luxxari and bought himself a new one. Here!' he rescued two of the photos from Maddy's discard pile and waved them at her. One of the Luxxari – a classic, these days – and one of himself, dressed in the St Lucre's uniform, standing next to Pete. But Maddy took one look at his cap, emblazoned with the school's crest of a gilded bull fighting a bear, his filigree-piped blazer, and his shiny black shoes, and let out a sigh.

'Try to think of something more relatable,' she pleaded.

What could be more relatable than a youthful indiscretion involving a luxury sports car?

'So you're not going to put any of my car photos in?'

'These?' Maddy inspected a picture of Hugh leaning in what he imagined was a sexy pose against a late model Luxxari. 'These are fine. Better than fine. Aspirational, even. But all the pictures of you lounging around your family's palatial home in your private school uniform? They've got to go. They just highlight the gulf between you and the reader. No one will buy your book unless they can see themselves in your story. Unless they believe that they, too, can become a CEO and one day have all those luxuries.'

Hugh snorted. He had gotten where he had through sheer force of will. Good old fashioned determination and willpower. How was it his fault if 'normal people' didn't have any stickability? Any – what was it his papa used to call it? 'Gumption'.

'How is that fair?' he protested. 'Noel Skum has pictures of his rocket in his book!'

'Sure, but his company built it. How many pictures are there of his father's diamond mine?

Hugh pouted.

'One last thing-' Maddy said. 'The title.'

Hugh nodded eagerly. 'I've been thinking we should go for something a bit edgy. Like, *The CEO Stripped Bare*.'

Maddy's face looked just like Pete's after a night out on the hard stuff.

'I don't think that's such a good idea,' she said. 'After the allegations.'

She had a point, Hugh supposed. Still, he maintained, all he had been doing was airing out after an unfortunate blunder in the executive bathroom. There was nothing sexual about him sitting at his desk half-naked. Alyssa had completely misread the situation. Yet again.

'I've got a list of suggestions here,' Maddy pushed a sheet of paper across the desk. 'What do you think?'

Hugh needed to look no further than the first item on the list – exhibiting one of the traits he prided himself on as a CEO – rapid decision making: *A Way to Build a Company, a Way to Build a Life,*

and a Way to Build a Unified Way: A Memoir of Hugh J. Richardson,
CEO of CGM.

Sure, it was the longest title by far. But didn't he deserve a long one?
It had everything. Business. Life. A hint of patriotism. Perfect.

'I'll see you tomorrow,' Maddy said, slinging her bag over her
shoulder.

'Tomorrow?'

'I'm going to shadow you, remember? Get a sense of your work day.
Maybe even take a few shots of you on the job. For the book.'

For the book. That's right. That was one thing Hugh hadn't been able
to find – any pictures of himself appearing to work. Signing papers.
Talking into a phone. As Maddy stepped into the elevator, he racked
his brain, trying to think of how to represent what it was that he did as
Chief Executive Officer of CGM.

He pulled Skum's biography from the shelf once more, skipping
straight past all the boring anecdotes from his childhood and accounts
of the supermodels he'd dated. At least, that's what Hugh imagined
all those pages he'd never read contained. At last he arrived at the
well-thumbed glossy pages.

Of course, it was easy if you were Skum. Even if he didn't invent any
of it himself, Skum could at least pose next to things his workers
made. Hugh didn't even know the names of half of CGM's
subsidiaries, let alone what their employees did.

But Maddy had made it quite clear that the work-related photos for
his book should show him actually *doing* something. Pouring through
CGM's listings of subsidiaries, struggling to find one which did
anything more exciting than shuffle money around, last week Hugh
had come across Freshwater Streams, and jumped at the chance to
tour what he imagined to be a fancy bottled water plant while wearing
a hardhat and looking important. Unfortunately, Freshwater Streams

was the region's premier sewage treatment plant.

Come to think of it, the smell was such that Hugh was certain that his face would have contorted in every single photo.

He stopped on one of the well-worn photo pages. There was Skum, smirking in a cowboy hat on a movie set. In a leather jacket, watching the launch of one of his rockets. In one of his signature black shirts, holding up some device. Shirtless on one of his superyachts. Standing, arms folded, in front of some enormous machine. Flashing the victory sign as he walked up the red carpet, one of his wives glittering on his other arm.

Hugh wasn't sure if it was Skum's first wife, or his second (who was also his third). Yet another way in which Skum out-scored him. Hugh had gotten the divorce part all right, but he was yet to find the next Mrs. Richardson. Perhaps he could take a leaf out of his hero's book, and see if Bambi would take him back.

He walked over to Alyssa's former desk and rifled through her drawers, at last finding a pen. Standard company issue cheap blue ink, they were easier for chewing on than his. The pens people gave Hugh were cold and hard. They had metal barrels that chipped his teeth, necessitating further expensive dental work at the company's expense.

After the company restricted staff to one pen per year, Alyssa had started complaining that every time he destroyed one of her pens, she had to buy another. Eventually, she'd taken to hiding her pens in all sorts of bizarre places. The drawer containing her shoes. A box marked 'personal,' which Hugh discovered contained sanitary products. And even, Hugh suspected, on her waistband. In fact, Hugh maintained he had merely been testing this theory when Alyssa accused him of patting her on the behind.

He returned to his executive ergonomic chair. It was rated for up to eight hours' continuous work, though Hugh's own behind had never come close to testing that. Crushing the plastic ends of the last of Alyssa's pens under the might of his newly implanted molars, he called Pete.

'You going to this thing tonight?' Hugh asked, the phone handset digging into his shoulder. Now that Alyssa was no longer here to show him how to set it to speakerphone, Hugh was a lost cause.

Pete laughed. 'You've gotta be kidding!'

Hugh was kidding. No CEO worth their $38 mil a year (in Hugh's case, soon to be $52 mil) would be stupid enough to attend an event titled 'Workers vs. CEOs' to be streamed live on the internet.

Come to think of it, Pete had taken part in something called 'Workers vs. CEOs' several years back. But that had been a charity wrestling match, not some town hall discussion of working conditions. Hugh couldn't recall exactly what the charity was – the cause of an event was never really important.

He suspected Pete had only taken part because he'd been rejected from *Secret CEO*, the show where CEOs – usually famous ones, like Noel Skum, or Johnny Cheesy – dressed up as rank-and-file employees, mopping the factory floor or flipping burgers.

Though he'd never admitted as much to Pete, Hugh had also been rejected from *Secret CEO*. He'd applied in one of the later seasons, after they'd already exhausted the pool of big names and big companies. He'd passed the first trial all right. None of Hugh's employees recognized him even when he was walking around in his signature suit. But Hugh was rejected at the audition interview, after he failed to identify any of the tasks his workers might perform on a daily basis, and what sort of disguise he might wear.

It was a shame, really. Hugh had always felt a special thrill whenever he'd dress up as the air-conditioning repairman, or put on their pool boy's accent, back when he and Bambi were still together. At one point, he'd even asked Marshall, his hot-shot lawyer, to see if there was any way of forcing the producer's hand. He wondered what had ever become of that.

Of course, Cheesy had his very own show – Hugh's favorite – *You're Terminated*. On occasions, Hugh wished he was more personally involved in the running of CGM. That he got to sit across from an employee, face-to-face, like Cheesy did, and deliver a catch-phrase like "you're terminated". The personal touch. But every time there was right-sizing or restructuring to be done, Hugh brought in the professionals. External downsizers, who handled it for him.

Much to Pete's advantage, his employees had spent most of the 'Workers vs. CEOs' match fighting back their pent up rage. Not one had been game enough to punch him in the face, even though Hugh was secretly rooting for them to do so. Pete had an eminently punchable face. Instead, he ended the night bruiseless and celebrated for having raised several thousand dollars for – well, whatever it was. But tonight's event, Pete had assured him, would entail more verbal than physical sparring, organized by some activist politician. The one who tried to introduce those workplace reforms Hugh had spent hundreds of thousands lobbying against last year.

'They'll just be moaning on about maternity and sick leave.'

'Health insurance,' Hugh added, chuckling. 'And dental coverage!'

'Drug testing,' Pete continued, rehashing the tired old lines, 'Overtime pay, and pensions.'

'Don't forget outsourcing and automation!'

'Compensation for injuries. Access to the kitchen facilities, or software installation, or bathrooms without clocking in and out. The usual garbage,' Pete chuckled. 'I mean, what are we meant to say?'

'You tell me! I don't think anyone's going,' Hugh was already dreading the shareholder's meeting he had to attend – at least via video conference – tomorrow. He didn't need another public event to add to his stress. Sure, he'd commissioned an exceedingly expensive multimedia presentation in the hopes it would distract everyone from the fact that, once again, he wasn't showing up in person.

And sure, he usually got representatives from each of the company's subsidiaries to field shareholders' questions. Even so, alternating between dynamic and responsible facial expressions as the question demanded was hard work.

Fortunately for Hugh, attendance at annual meetings was in decline. CGM wasn't the kind of company that held meetings with hot dog stands and pop stars. It was more of a cut-sandwiches-and-photocopied-info-sheets-with-free-pens company, and Hugh was grateful for that. All he ever had to do was write a letter – usually a half-page did it, with some sort of gaff about how they were all a big happy family, players on the same team – pose for a headshot, and smile on stage. Or into his webcam.

You could judge the profitability of CGM over any given year by the size of Hugh's smile. They were inversely correlated. The more teeth Hugh showed, the lower the return. An exuberant smile, he hoped, would prevent many of the investors from turning towards the back pages of the report, and looking over the less-than-stellar numbers in any great detail.

That was why Hugh invested so much in his dental work – or rather, he supposed, the company had. After all, why shouldn't he invoice the company for his cosmetic dentistry when it was for the company's benefit that he'd had it done? All those days off work in the chair to straighten and whiten – and lying around the resort afterwards to recover. No one could deny that straightness and whiteness were vital when it came to being a CEO, and Hugh strove to exude CEO-ness in his company photographs.

Come to think of it, Hugh couldn't remember the photographer visiting this year. Normally, they sent someone – dressed all in black, with arty stubble or jaunty glasses and an asymmetric haircut– to scale the CGM building, riding the elevator with his equipment all the way to the lofty heights of Hugh's 60th floor office to take a few shots, always from the same angle. Hugh had a definite 'good side', though he relied on Alyssa to remind him which side it was.

The photographer always brought what Hugh called his 'generic CEO background'. It was different to the sort of bright white or blue-green blur of generic employee photos. Instead, the background had a kind of browny-gray dappled texture that made Hugh look slightly older and more serious, yet, at the same time, warm and upstanding. Hugh wished he could have his office walls painted to match.

'I've gotta go,' Hugh said, flipping back to the start of the shareholder's report, his favorite section, where the pages were glossy and colorful, and the words were short and few, but printed in big letters, like his essays at St. Lucre's – at least, the ones he'd written himself after the master found out he'd been paying Pete to write them. 'Something's come up.' He hung up the phone, then poured over each page carefully.

To be honest, Hugh hadn't been all that concerned when the photographer hadn't knocked on his door this year. There was a strong possibility he'd just been out of the office and missed him – Hugh spent only a handful of days in the office each year. But he had also secretly hoped that the company had just decided to go with last year's head shot. That's what he was planning for the book jacket. Hugh had noticed a few extra lines around his eyes this year, a few more grey hairs – thanks to his divorce, or more truthfully, the subsequent wrangling over their shared assets. Trying to retain his wealth – and his rank on the *Fobbs 400 Rich List* – had consumed most of Hugh's attention over the last twelve months.

He didn't need the money. There was nothing more crass than wanting something simply because you needed it in Hugh's book. Nor did he begrudge Bambi the money. In fact, for a fleeting moment, headlines trumpeting 'One of the largest divorce settlements in history' had danced through his head.

What better way to show how rich, powerful – and yet, deeply moral and upstanding – he was? Then, he'd thought to actually look up how much he would have to give away in order to attract such press coverage, and realized he'd have to go into debt several times over to even compete with the current record holder, and decided it wasn't worth it.

His money was his life work. His legacy. The legacy of his family, for generations. He couldn't let his wife and bratty kids diminish that. Yes, Hugh decided, fighting for every last penny was not only the right course of action – it was the only moral one.

As soon as he was old enough to come into his family money, Hugh had obsessively checked *Fobb's*. He substituted his rank on the *Rich List* for his rank on *Commando Force X: Friendly Fire*. Money was, after all, the points system in the game of life, and Hugh's rankings in *Fobb's* were always better than on *Commando Force X*. At least, until Pete showed him how to buy supply crates. Hugh's childhood would have been very different had you been able to pay to win back then.

His heart began to beat faster as he searched his memory. Come to think of it, he couldn't remember Alyssa getting him to sign off on an updated version of his bio this year, either. Normally, Hugh didn't care much, and Alyssa just submitted the same one he'd been using since he landed the top job at CGM. But this year of all years, Hugh had something to be proud of.

This year, Hugh had made perhaps the most important executive decision in the history of CGM. The introduction of the software system that was going to completely change the company.

In fact, it was when she tried to interfere with the introduction of the AutoAutomator software, that Lila really got under Hugh's skin.

Still, he'd managed to get the lawyers to sign off on the rollout in record time, and the benefits of the AutoAutomator software made up the bulk of Hugh's letter to the shareholders this year. Alyssa, he assumed, had passed his draft to one of the professional writers the company outsourced things to, to 'massage his narrative'. After all, Hugh's letters were much more than a simple communique to the company's fellow owners. They were one of the firm's most important forms of marketing.

CEO letters impacted stock price, pure and simple. Sure, the vast majority of stocks were held by institutions with highly paid analysts, and more importantly, powerful computers. But there were still individual investors – the bane of Hugh's existence, when it came to the annual meetings, with their impudent questions about why the company refused to divest from fossil tobacco, or gambling oil, or whatever it was.

And individuals tended to place a much higher emphasis on the CEO's letter than perhaps they should.

But Hugh couldn't remember seeing a final version.

Hugh was not a businessman of letters. Even after the professional hacks worked their magic on them, Hugh knew his letters would never be collected into leather bound volumes and read from by future generations as the epitome of business writing over the last century. They would never be studied at prestigious universities, quoted by MBA students, or excerpted in *Top CEO Magazine* or *Fobbs*.

And that was exactly as intended.

After all, it was easy to write a good letter – one that was insightful, educative, entertaining even – if you had good performance to reflect on.

What took real skill was the wrangling of a decent letter from a year of lackluster – or more often, poor results.

Hugh's letters took the form of a standard template that used promotional language to highlight the successes of the company while glossing over its failures. And of course, they were always the company's failures, not his, though the paycheck was Hugh's alone.

Just like horoscope writers who take care to only predict the future and never repeat their past predictions for fact-checking, Hugh's letters never reflected on how the company had failed to meet the previous year's targets.

But Hugh had an even more effective tactic than the psychics and astrologers who dissuade people from rereading old horoscopes by telling them it would bring bad fortune.

By writing such unmemorable, bland letters which no one in their right mind would waste filing cabinet or even hard drive space retaining, Hugh could pretty much guarantee that none of the shareholders would retain a copy of his previous statements to measure his current performance against.

On occasion, he might point out something he had actually achieved, as was his intent this year, with the AutoAutomator roll out. But more often than not, and especially in the bad years, Hugh was careful to distance himself from any insinuation of responsibility.

'At CGM, we play as a team, making the whole bigger than the sum of its parts, resulting in a more holistic and active approach,' he might write. Or, 'Our company is uniquely positioned in that our team provides a broad array of products and services for a diverse, fully-integrated marketplace.'

Meaningless drivel, but it sounded good.

The key was to blame any failures on external, even global market forces. Meanwhile, Hugh attributed any successes to his own superb captaining of the corporate ship. His own steady hand on the tiller.

Unlike the financial section of the report, (which CGM, like every other company, hid up the back, printed in microscopic, monochromatic font, on a grade of paper expertly designed to make your hands dry and your skin crack), the CEO's letter, and its accompanying glossy images, were essentially unregulated.

There were no rules about what a CEO could claim, so long as they weren't outright lies, Hugh supposed. Still, he certainly had friends on the board who'd gotten away with suggesting their own companies had had a 'stellar year' when their financial reports showed losses for the first time in half a decade.

Nor were there rules about what a CEO had to disclose in their letter – unlike the rest of the report, where, for example, it was now mandated that companies inform the public how much their CEOs were compensated relative to their median employees.

Hugh's own compensation package had come in at over 400 times that of the median employee at CGM. Not that Hugh really knew who the median employee was. Still, his friends in fast food and manufacturing came off looking worse.

The CEO of McKing's, Hugh knew, earned more than 3,000 times what they paid their pimple-faced counter attendants in a year. Deborah, the CEO of ToyStar, made nearly 5,000 times what they paid their foreign manufacturers.

The introduction of this new regulation was the first time Hugh was glad he had to pay his workers more than child or foreign slaves. He still felt inadequate comparing packages with the other members of the board, who were all CEOs of megacorporations themselves. The CEO-vs-worker ratio was just another metric for them to compete on. Another set of points.

The inability to dissuade investors from looking too much at the figures by using unpleasant paper was only one of the reasons Hugh had a strong distaste for electronic reports. Giving investors annual reports online also enabled them to search for specific facts or figures. They could even use the zoom tool, counteracting the very reason CGM printed the financial details so small.

An added bonus of using poor quality paper was that any overzealous investor scrutinizing the numbers might easily mistake a decimal place for just another fault in the page, and assume the profits were one hundred times larger than they were.

Hugh leafed through the report once more, swirling his drink anxiously. The first few pages were splashed with sunny green fields and happy, white-teethed people. He never saw much sense in photos like these. It seemed juvenile, almost like a children's picture-book, or a women's magazine, and he couldn't see the relevance. It wasn't as if CGM dealt with farming or dentistry.

At least, Hugh didn't think they had any agricultural or medtech firms in their portfolio. But his advisors told him that investors were willing to buy stock at higher prices on sunny rather than rainy days. That images with green and nature calm people down. And that seeing other people smile made them feel more positive and trusting.

Some study – there was always a study with these advisors – had shown that people were much less critical when primed with a green rather than a red cover. The last thing CGM wanted was for anyone to go through their figures with a critical eye.

Finally, Hugh found it. 'A letter from the CEO'.

He leaned back in his chair to reread the letter. He couldn't really remember exactly what he'd written. Truth be told, he couldn't really remember writing it at all. His vague recollection of passing the draft to Alyssa could just as easily have been a memory from last year, or the year before that.

Things had been hectic with the AutoAutomator roll-out. True, the roll-out didn't require much involvement on Hugh's part other than several all-expenses-paid trips to the AutoAutomator head office with the other board members who'd decided to try it out. But the whole thing had coincided with the negotiation of his divorce settlement, and honestly, Hugh wouldn't have been surprised if the letter had slipped his mind entirely.

He was relieved to see that he'd been more on top of matters than he thought.

The letter was brilliant.

It skated neatly around all of the issues CGM had faced over the past year, most notably Hugh's own 'indiscretions' which had led to not only several sexual harassment lawsuits but his second divorce.

It provided a handful of cherry-picked, promising-looking statistics from the financial report, all seasoned with meaningless yet inspiring-sounding platitudes about diversity and corporate responsibility and company culture.

It was a letter crafted to give the reader the impression they'd already read everything of value. They'd already seen enough numbers, and there was absolutely no need to continue reading.

Indeed, why bother pawing through all those dry ledgers and tables at the back, when you could pick up the phone and call your broker, or click on your screen and buy some more CGM right now?

But it wasn't Hugh's letter.

The first clue was that it didn't mention the AutoAutomator rollout even once.

And the second, more telling clue, was that at the bottom of the page, where it should have read, 'Hugh J. Richardson, CEO' instead, it said 'Mike J. Guy, CEO'.

CHAPTER 2

Hugh stared at the enormous flourishing signature, even bigger and bolder than his own already cavalier autograph. And there, next to the green call-outs with their uplifting arrows, which, Hugh knew, predisposed investors to positive associations with value, was a photograph of this Mike J. Guy.

He was in a charcoal suit, just like the one Hugh's stylist always had him wear. 'Charcoal's more approachable than jet black,' Zach said, 'yet more formal and trustworthy than light gray.'

Mike's shoulder was even rotated slightly away from the camera in what Hugh thought of as his signature pose but which, in fact, 90% of the nation's top CEOs used in their head shots. He wore a blue-and-red striped tie, just like Hugh's – it was a point of pride that he wore the company's colors for his professional portraits. And he was smiling a smile that exposed the same precisely calculated amount of teeth as Hugh practiced in the mirror each morning.

Hugh hit redial. Surely Pete would know what all this was about. He was on the CGM board.

They couldn't have replaced him, Hugh thought as he waited for Pete to answer. Pete would have said something. He'd seemed completely normal on the phone.

Then again, maybe that was part of the board's strategy. Have him leave without the sort of fuss Parker made the first two times he was fired.

Maybe that's why Pete said nothing, to make less trouble for the board. Why the publisher had downgraded his book to an autobiography, so they could capitalize on the lurid details of his failure once he'd signed the release. Why the company had let him keep coming into the office.

Hugh's heart felt as though it was going to burst through his chest. Why wasn't Pete answering? He hit redial again.

If he was lucky, once the annual meeting was over, the company would ship him off to a big villa in a tropical locale. One with a pool and massages and white-coated 'doctors' who'd pump him full of the drugs Parker's company made. Where they'd send him off to 'equine-assisted therapy'.

Hugh rifled through his drawer, looking for the brochures of those executive-level fifty-grand-a-month facilities he'd poured over, back when he'd been arrested for drunk driving. For a while, it looked like he might have to do a stint in jail if he didn't undergo treatment. Fortunately, he'd gotten away with a $5,000 fine.

It was his legal defense that had cost him. Still, William Marshall was the best in the business, and you got what you paid for. Marshall was even the one who'd hooked him up with that expert who clinched the deal in his divorce proceedings.

Yes, it would suit the board quite nicely to have him holed up somewhere like that, Hugh supposed. Meanwhile, they'd take away everything that meant anything to him. For the longest time, work was the only thing going right in Hugh's life.

He took a deep breath, then a long swig, and forced himself to try and think clearly. This, Hugh realized, was very likely an oversight. A mistake of some sort.

They couldn't fire him. He was the face of the CGM.

Heck, he *was* CGM.

It had to be a mistake. A simple slip-up at the printers. They'd inserted the wrong file, the letter page from some other company, and printed it up as part of the CGM package by mistake.

Hugh glanced back at the letter as he continued to wait for Pete to pick up.

No. The letter definitely mentioned CGM by name several times. And there was a bunch of facts and figures relating to the company which Hugh couldn't judge the accuracy of, but which certainly looked plausible.

Maybe it was an issue with the writers. Maybe they shouldn't have outsourced something as important as drafting his letter to a couple of professional corporate-speak bullshit artists, like they did with advertising and social media relations.

That was it. It was very likely, Hugh assured himself, that the hacks Alyssa had sent his letter to had used the same template for all their clients. They'd inserted the CGM data, but simply forgotten to change the name from their last client to Hugh J. Richardson at the end.

Maybe it was only his copy that had this mistake. As the CEO, Hugh would have been provided with one of the earliest copies of the report. A copy which, he admitted, had been sitting on his desk for weeks beneath his well-thumbed golf magazines, and his pile of newspapers. He used to get Alyssa to iron them for him each morning, but since she'd been gone, they remained rolled up on his desk.

Surely the error would have been caught before distribution to the board members – and more importantly, the stock exchange, and hence, the public at large.

'Shoot!' Pete finally answered.

'Have you read the CGM report yet?' Hugh had no time for pleasantries. Not that Pete ever offered any. Still, that's what old school friends were for.

'What is this, you want to copy my book report?' Pete chuckled. Hugh could just imagine his face, gloating while he reminisced about their days at St. Lucre's. It wasn't as if Pete was any better at writing than he was. Hugh had only ever outsourced his work to Pete because he couldn't be bothered doing it himself. And Pete, Hugh long suspected, had pawned off the work on the tutor his parents hired from some fancy institution overseas, pocketing a tidy profit from Hugh's allowance along the way.

'Page seven. What do you see?'

'I don't know,' Pete said. Hugh listened for the sounds of him rummaging through his drawers. Pete kept a pristine office – or rather, his assistant did. There was nothing on Pete's desk but a slender laptop and a smooth paperweight whose purpose Hugh could never discern, as Pete never had any paper on his desk. But Pete's drawers, off-limits to his assistant, were always a mess. Once, when Hugh asked him for a pen, Pete took fifteen minutes to find one among the half-eaten candy bars, three-quarters empty whisky bottles, and dirty magazines. Though he was slightly more technologically competent than Hugh when it came to games, Pete was old-fashioned in his other tastes. 'I don't know where I put my copy.'

Typical Pete. 'Go on the website then!'

'Ah-ha!' Thank goodness he didn't take too long. Hugh was in no mood to wait. His heart still felt as if it might burst through his sternum at any moment.

'Page seven, page seven...' Pete muttered under his breath. Hugh could hear him scrolling. 'Looks like a pretty standard letter to me, old boy! So what?'

'What does it say down the bottom?' Hugh squeezed his eyes together as he waited for Pete's response, trying to imagine his name in print.

'Mike J. Guy, CEO. Hey, wait! Shouldn't that be your name there?'

'Of course it should!' Hugh shouted. He slammed his fist, the resultant sound unsatisfyingly muffled by his leather desk pad. He needed to control himself. Maybe Pete was just playing dumb. Maybe he knew something Hugh didn't.

Perhaps an extraordinary meeting had been called, and Hugh had been voted out. He'd missed several board meetings in the last few months. His calendar had been so packed with the divorce settlement hearings, the ongoing resolution of his harassment proceedings (which Marshall had assured him he could settle out of court and off the record if he threw enough money at it), his golf days, and of course, the meetings for all the other boards he was on. Hugh had accumulated quite the collection of board positions, trading private jets and enormous compensation packages with his friends as though they were baseball cards.

But surely someone would have told him something. After all, he'd been coming into the office every day – well, most days, when he wasn't golfing. Or at court. Or down at his summer house.

Pete, of all people, would have said something. They were buddies. They golfed together. They were best man at each other's weddings, and Hugh was godfather to Pete's kids.

They were on each others' company boards, for heaven's sake! Was there any bond more sacred?

'Is there anything I should know?' Hugh asked, trying to control his voice. 'Has the board,' he swallowed the lump in his throat, 'replaced me?'

'Replaced you? You've gotta be kidding!'

'There hasn't been any discussion of my...' Hugh's voice stuck in his throat, like a fish bone, 'performance?' The word made him feel impotent, as if he needed to take some little blue pill to return his firm resolution and explosive business savvy.

'Of course not!' Pete paused. 'Well, I mean, I didn't attend the last couple of meetings – and I was pretty hungover the one before that,' he admitted. 'But someone would have said something, right?'

Hugh said nothing. The imagined fish bone was cutting into his throat again.

'Deborah at least,' Pete continued. 'She's at all the meetings. And we had dinner with her last week, remember. She seemed normal enough, didn't she?'

Hugh exhaled. Indeed, he hadn't detected anything off about Deborah's conduct last week. At least, no more off than usual. It was hard to tell with women, given all their mood swings.

'Why don't you ask her?'

Hugh frowned. He hated talking to Deborah at the best of times. The only reason she was on the board was the same reason Kim was – to shut up the shareholders who kept banging on about diversity. In fact, had Kim been who Hugh was expecting, Deborah would never have made it to the board. Based on the name, and a poorly photocopied headshot, Hugh had thought he was appointing an Asian lesbian, when in reality, Kim Park was a white man with a bad haircut.

As always, Deborah picked up on the third ring.

'Deb! Have you got the CGM report handy?'

'Sure,' Hugh could visualize her reaching over to the standing file she kept on the left-hand side of her desk. 'What's up?'

'Page seven,' Hugh repeated, the receiver almost slipping from his increasingly clammy palm. He listened intently as she flipped through the thick, glossy pages at the start of the report. Hugh never had to look at the financials to tell how well his, or any of his colleagues' companies had done that year. As soon as he felt the thickness and saw the glossiness of the pages of the annual report, Hugh knew with greater accuracy than he could ever glean from a spreadsheet. CGM always sprang for high-quality paper, especially in the bad years. It gave off a calculated aura of performance, designed to counteract the lackluster figures. The thicker the paper, Hugh's mantra went, the thinner the margins.

'What's going on?' Deborah asked.

'You don't know either?'

'You quit?'

'No!' Hugh exclaimed – then fell silent. Maybe he had. He'd been under a lot of pressure lately. The doctor had upped his sleeping pills, and his antidepressant prescription. And he'd been drinking more than he had since his last arrest. And doing a little recreational on the side with Pete.

'Shit!' Deborah's voice pulled Hugh back to the conversation. 'I'm not in here either!'

'What do you mean?'

'On the board members page.'

Hugh turned to the double-page spread that featured head shots of each of the board members. Underneath each was a brief spiel about their backgrounds – carefully omitting any mention of the various competing companies they also ran or served on the boards of.

He hadn't noticed anything unusual about the board members page on his first flip through. As he stared at the page again in full, he still didn't. For years, Hugh and his friends had feared being replaced by a motley crew of 'diversity' hires like Deborah. But what Hugh saw was the same old sea of white against brown – upper-middle-aged upper-class white men with distinguishedly white-streaked hair against mottled brown-gray backgrounds.

When he looked at each photo individually, Hugh saw that Deb was right.

Her photo was nowhere to be seen.

It wouldn't be the first time the company had forgotten to include Deborah in the line-up. The first year her photo made it to the printers, they mistakenly identified her as Hugh's secretary. Initially, that made Hugh chuckle – until he realized what it might do to his reputation. It wouldn't do him any good to be seen as having such an unattractive secretary. That's why he'd hired Alyssa. She had a fine pair of legs – even if she was slow to refill the pens.

Ever since, Deborah's photo had been easy to spot – she had an irritating tendency to wear brightly colored blazers. It wasn't fair that women got to wear colors other than gray to work. Hugh didn't care one jot about expressing his personality through his attire. But he despised how Deborah's jackets distracted from his own photo, stealing his limelight.

'We're all gone!' Deborah spluttered.

Typical. Now that Deborah noticed her photo was missing she had to make a big deal out of it, as if she constituted the entire board. Sure, she did do eighty percent of what little work the board actually achieved. But there were other butts on the seats around the table, not just her own derriere, which, Hugh had noticed, was slightly lopsided. Hugh might not be good at faces, but he never forgot a behind.

But as he looked at each photo individually, Hugh saw that Deborah was right.

There was no photograph of Pete. Nor Kim. Nor Parker.

There were, however, two Johns, a Steven, two Davids, a James, and a Greg.

How had he missed this?

In Hugh's defense, the double-paged spread – the 'centerfold', as Pete laughingly called it – was virtually indistinguishable from the one published in CGM's previous report. Or the one before that. In fact, it looked the same as the board member's page of every board Hugh sat on. Almost exclusively white, middle-aged-to-older males, and most with a good crop of hair, or at least, a decent toupee. The spread was, in short, a grown-up version of the St. Lucre's Private Boys' Grammar yearbook.

Sure, Hugh had seen plenty of reports suggesting there should be more diversity in corporate boards. In fact, he paid those reports more attention than he paid to most reports, because they often featured portraits of exotic women in low-cut business suits. But it wasn't as if CGM was in any way unique. Only around half of companies worldwide had even a single woman on their boards. And even in Hugh's own supposedly egalitarian and free country, boards were only getting whiter and maler.

Hugh hung up the phone without saying goodbye, and stared at the spread.

It could only mean one thing.

If it wasn't only Hugh who had been replaced, then this wasn't about him.

It wasn't about the scandals he'd caused. It wasn't about the time he'd taken off work. It wasn't about his drinking. And it wasn't even about the one thing Hugh had feared most: a lack of 'diversity'. This new board was as pasty and testosterone-fuelled (or at least, Parker's patented PharmaX testosterone-replacement-fuelled) as ever.

It was about the company.

There must have been a hostile takeover.

For the first time in a long time, Hugh decided, he would attend the stockholder's meeting in person tomorrow.

CHAPTER 3

As always, the annual meeting was on a Wednesday morning. As always, it was held inside an enormous glass-and-steel convention center in the middle of some industrial estate, and as always, it was surrounded by protesters.

'Surrounded' was too generous a descriptor. What Hugh meant was that there were eight or nine people out front, half of them dressed in what he supposed was their idea of 'corporate attire': ill-fitting black suits that weren't last season's or even last decade's, but last generation's at best, paired with ratty sneakers. He supposed these jobless morons didn't own any proper shoes. Each held a faux chainsaw constructed of cardboard and plywood.

The other four or five protesters, Hugh could only assume were meant to represent trees and some sort of forest animal. Their poorly-assembled costumes were worse than the ones on display at his son's kindergarten play, the year St. Lucre's ill-advisedly encouraged the students to make their own outfits. Hugh shuddered at the memory of seeing Hugh J. Richardson Jnr. IV on stage, spray-painted pantyhose stretched over his arms and a bulbous papier-mâché hat glued to his head.

As Hugh and the rest of the board approached the building, the protesters in suits began to mock-attack the tree and animal protesters.

Hugh knew how this went. Soon they'd unfurl a banner of some sort, claiming one of CGM's many subsidiaries was 'murdering' whatever the hell those animals were supposed to be. Hugh slowed his pace, maneuvering his body so that he was shielded by Parker, who was easily the largest of the group, and Deborah, whose jacket, frankly, would only be improved by a splash of red paint. As they walked past, Hugh squeezed his eyes closed, bracing for the inevitable bucket.

But it didn't happen.

Maybe this year's protesters were more civilized than what he'd seen of last year's over the video link. Hugh remembered there had been people in masks holding up signs about the one percent – the 'cream of the crop', as Hugh liked to think of himself – and something about better wages for the 99%. Although he hadn't been able to make out individual faces, Hugh had to imagine Lila was there, with her dyed hair and her union buddies. They'd tried to set up their filthy tents in the foyer, before security turfed them out onto the pavement.

Could you turf someone out onto pavement? Hugh wondered. He supposed it didn't really count if you were being hurled onto concrete or gravel instead of grass, but still, 'concreted' or 'pavemented' didn't sound right either. He'd have to ask Maddy.

In any case, Hugh was pleased to see that the number of protesters was down. Not because their relative absence signified a positive change in the company's image – it didn't – but because it meant all the time Hugh had gotten Alyssa to spend identifying cities with the worst public transit infrastructure as candidates to host the annual meeting was well spent.

Usually, when they bothered to attend the meeting in person at all, Hugh and the board were ushered in through a private corridor up the back – the 'discrete rear entrance' as Pete called it. But this time, Hugh wanted to make a dramatic entrance. To storm in – and to take this Mike J. Guy by storm.

A blast of frigid air hit Hugh as the automatic doors opened. The chill not only slapped his face and hands, but even penetrated his super 200 thread count Luxurio suit.

'It's like a morgue in here!' Pete complained. Hugh beamed. Only Parker, still sweating from his traipse across the parking lot and up the punishingly large number of stairs leading up to the building (another feature Hugh had asked Alyssa to look for), had any color left in his face.

Hugh's smile widened. Everything was as it should be.

The company had to fork out an extra forty grand to get the engineers in the week before to lower the minimum temperature the air-conditioning would go down to before triggering its emergency shutdown procedure. It was worth every penny.

Hugh couldn't imagine how anyone could sit through an entire meeting in this building, let alone stop their teeth chattering long enough to form any coherent questions. And if Alyssa's constant complaining was anything to go by, women felt the cold more than men, so the frigid atmosphere was a double bonus when it came to sieving people out.

'Welcome CGM Shareholders!'

For years, Hugh had looked at that electronic display with pride – via his webcam, or when he saw footage of the meeting after the fact. Seeing the company's logo up there was almost as good as seeing his own face or name up in lights. In a way, he supposed, it was his face, his name – or rather, his face and name belonged to the company.

Hugh swallowed, remembering why he was here. That Mike J. Guy must be around somewhere, gloating that it was his name and face in the company report, pacing around in the back room, eating Hugh's pastries and drinking Hugh's whisky.

'ID, please,' a security guard dressed in an enormous puffy jacket and a beanie prompted.

'You know who I am! I'm the CEO!'

The guard raised an eyebrow. 'Very funny. Now, show me some ID so we can keep this line moving. We're expecting a couple of hundred people today.'

'You think I don't know that?' Hugh exploded, though internally, he was thrilled. He and the board had a little competition every year, to see who could repel the most investors, and were it not for the fact that he couldn't get in to his own meeting, Hugh would be getting ready to count his winnings. 'I'm the CEO!'

He felt a hand on his shoulder. Pete. Hugh knew he was right – he had to calm down. That's why Pete was such a good friend. For all his jokes and jabs, Pete was always there for him in the hard times.

Hugh patted his pockets, desperate to find something with his name on it. His drivers license had been suspended months ago. Not that he really needed one. The company supplied him with a driver. His passport, of course, was in the safe.

'Here!' he said, dumping the contents of his leather wallet onto the table: a 'Very Important Member' card from his luxury 'gentlemen's club', his Platinum Gold level Patriot International Express card, the strip of paper the state had issued him when he forfeited his license, and an expired video rental membership card, testament to how little Hugh used his wallet. He had no need for cash, or even credit cards. Most places he went, Hugh just added his expenses to his tab, and Alyssa settled them later. At least, that's what he assumed. Now that she was gone, Hugh wasn't sure what happened.

The guard checked his list and nodded. 'Welcome. Thank you for choosing to invest with CGM'.

'I didn't choose to! I've been paid in these damned stocks for the past four years!' Hugh scowled as Deb and Kim got their passes. Even Parker was beginning to look chilly as he flashed his driver's license. Typical, Hugh thought. He would have to show off the fact that he still had a driver's license. And it wasn't as if Parker never drove under the influence. He just happened to own the labs that processed the blood tests.

Pete was up next.

'You're not on the list, sir.'

'What do you mean? Look! My name's right here!' Pete pointed at his own license.

'There's nothing wrong with your ID, sir, I can read it quite clearly. It's just that your name isn't on the list.'

'But I'm a board member.'

'Friends with this guy, are you?' The guard jerked a thumb towards Hugh. 'Look, I don't have time for this. You're name is not on the list of shareholders, and it's definitely not on the list of board members. This is a private meeting, for shareholders only.'

'Check again,' Kim intervened, securing his own pass around his neck. 'Pete should be on there.'

'I assure you, he's not. Now, if you have a copy of your stock certificate on you, you can show it to my colleague down there and she'll print you a temporary pass.'

Pete bit his lip. 'I'll catch up with you guys afterwards.'

'Come on!' Kim insisted. 'Don't let this asshole get the better of you. You've got your phone with you. Just show them your holdings and they'll be shitting bricks.'

Pete whispered something Hugh couldn't hear over the low hum of the airconditioning, and the high-pitched squeal of the fluorescent lights. Already, he could feel his head throbbing.

'What?'

'I don't own any.'

Hugh felt something twinge in his chest.

'I sold all of my shares,' Pete continued. 'Before the cut-off date.'

The fishbone returned to Hugh's throat. 'That's why you couldn't find the report?' he choked out. 'Why you weren't surprised you weren't on the board anymore?'

'I'll see you at the bar afterwards.' Pete turned and left.

CHAPTER 4

The stabbing in Hugh's chest grew worse. He filed into the meeting hall, gripping the rolled-up annual report in his hand as though he were about to swat a fly on his yacht.

It wasn't as if the company had been loyal to him.

Still, Pete selling off his shares was a clear vote of no confidence not only in the company, but in Hugh's leadership. Sure, Hugh had only recently had his accountant file the forms required to report Hugh's own sale of a good chunk of his shares. He squeaked in just before the cut-off date and just after the financial newspapers went to press. But this was different.

Pete was supposed to be his friend.

His betrayal stung Hugh almost as much as not seeing his name in the annual report had.

The meeting room was full of mostly empty seats. Only a handful of serious investors, plus the usual crackpots with an axe to grind had bothered to show up. Clearly, the years of inconvenient locations and scheduling, frosty greetings and even frostier climate control, cuts to shareholder perks, and limits imposed upon Q&As had had their desired effect. Hugh almost glowed with pride. Then he realized it would be Mike J. Guy, not him, who would be getting credit with the board for these unprecedented levels of apathy. For the disengagement that allowed the controlling interests to continue to control their interests.

Hugh squinted as he glanced up at the stage, the screens even larger and brighter than he remembered. Two long tables up front, a podium in the center. The doors to the side, he supposed, led through to the showroom, where a variety of vendors were getting ready to show off whatever products and services the company's collection of smaller companies were currently producing. If indeed they were producing anything at all.

Over his relatively short and extremely inattentive tenure at CGM, even Hugh had noticed that most of the companies that actually did anything had been shifted overseas. All of the firm's recent acquisitions tended to have names like 'Real-time Aggregate Partners', 'Global Interface Solutions', 'Ubiquitous Supply-chain Management', 'Group Direct Development' or 'Central Dynamic Assurance'.

Next year, Hugh had hoped to man a booth of his own in the showroom. Well, not a booth, but to sit in a big chair up on a platform, where he could sign autographs. Skum was always milling about with his adoring crowd, posing for photos. Hugh knew CGM wasn't that sort of a company, but even Kim and Parker had booths at their company's shows. Of course, they both had books out already. Parker was probably the biggest celebrity of the group, Hugh thought with a streak of jealousy.

Last year, he'd taken home the 'Most Overpaid CEO of the Year' award, handed out by some do-gooder non-profit Hugh never bothered to remember the name of. There was no actual certificate or anything, but Parker had framed the cover of the report, which featured a photoshopped image of him, with dollar coins replacing his eyes, his tie patterned with greenbacks. Sales of his book had shot up after that.

Hugh had even been practicing his signature, signing the front page of all of the management books and celebrity biographies that lined his office walls, making sure his pen didn't obscure the title, or worse, the author name. Just like he used to practice coloring inside the lines at kindergarten – the last time he'd taken his schooling seriously.

It was the first time he'd opened any of the books in his office, other than Skum's well-worn volume, and Hugh had been rather annoyed to find that Kim had already autographed his own book.

He took a seat next to Parker. The chair was hard and plastic, and made him feel cheap, and somehow, even colder than he already felt. His back hurt. He choked back a cough as the air grew thick with the scent of layered aftershave, SpeedPuma Ultra antiperspirant, and the sticky smell of energy drinks.

He couldn't wait to get out of this room.

Hugh looked around for a donut or a sandwich of some kind, but saw nothing other than a single vat of coffee with some cheap plastic cups pushed into a corner. Pete would be disappointed – he was a donut fiend. Then Hugh remembered that Pete was a no good, dirty, lying, disloyal scumbag who didn't deserve a donut.

The lack of donuts was presumably in keeping with the company's 'fiscally responsible' narrative. A few candy bars or ham-and-cheese sandwiches wouldn't break the bank. But Hugh knew that the story you told was more important than the figures on the spreadsheet. At least, when those figures weren't very good. And that's all this was. A story. A great big show.

As Hugh knew from the few meetings he'd attended in his time as both a CEO and a member of other companies' boards, it was the companies that were performing the worst, and were most in need of belt-tightening, that were most likely to distract their investors with extravagant gift bags, barista coffee, and celebrity musical acts. Then again, you could manipulate people's access to drinks and snacks to all sorts of ends.

He remembered the first year they'd cut back on catering, in the aftermath of the worst market crash in a generation. Heck, in several. He'd explained to the room of terrified investors and nerve-stricken portfolio managers that this was part of the company's response to the recent crisis, and begged for their understanding. Of course, it was all for show. The government bailouts after this, and every subsequent real estate crash, natural disaster, or pandemic invariably meant CGM was in a far better position post 'crisis' than it was predicted to be before. A few strategically placed political 'donations' to both sides guaranteed that.

At any rate, CGM's catering costs for the annual meeting were always negligible. The sandwiches were outsourced to the inmates of whatever prison happened to be closest to that year's venue. And the candy bars and cookies came from a discount wholesaler that dealt in expired ex-vending machine stock.

Hugh chuckled as he remembered the weeks Alyssa would spend at her desk, carefully scratching out the consume-before date on each of the sweets. She always looked annoyed when he snuck a bar from the pile she'd already worked on. Any excess left after the meeting – and there was always excess, as nobody who took one dusty cookie or melted-and-reset chocolate ever went back for a second – was donated to the homeless and written off at full retail value, netting the company a nice little tax return.

Hugh's speech that year – telling the masses they wouldn't be getting their triangle sandwiches or their mini chocolate bars – was the only speech he'd ever made that received a round of applause. Even better, the shareholders voted in an overwhelming majority to approve his pay rise for the following year.

All because he'd denied them their cookies, and creamer for their coffees.

The biggest bonus of limiting the food available was that it dissuaded a good number of the crackpots from attending. Hugh was sure they only ever came for the free feed. Of course, they had to have some amount of money to own stocks in the company. But they were the sort who always wore t-shirts with holes in them and dirty sneakers, and drove cars that still had cassette players.

Some of the protesters out front were better dressed.

What was the point of having money, Hugh wondered, if nobody could tell you had it?

Of course, the austerity measures were never applied to the C-level execs. In some back room, Hugh knew, there would be mountains of pastries and lakes of coffee – plus a few stronger drinks.

He felt a pang of something – hunger, or, more likely, jealousy.

Not only did this Mike J. Guy have his job, but he was eating Hugh's pastries too. The ones with the swirl of raisins and almonds that he got Alyssa to order. No doubt he was sitting in Hugh's chair. With some young thing powdering his nose so it wouldn't shine under the spotlight. Straightening his collar so it looked crisp for the press release.

With a loud fanfare, the lights dimmed, and a video lit up the screens.

It was the presentation Hugh had commissioned. Fancy computer animations. Inspirational phrases on alternately calming and stimulating backgrounds. And a little spiel about himself at the end.

Of course, they'd replaced that part.

'Introducing Mike Guy!' the speakers blared instead. The asshole's face was on the screen, looking over Hugh, leering at him almost. Mocking him. Hugh felt the tightness in his chest again.

'Michael J. Guy is CGM's most dynamic CEO yet. Mike has used his time so far at CGM to close the loop in both B2B and B2C best practices, and to build CGM's capabilities and core competencies in content marketing, granular innovation, and holistic knowledge process outsourcing by focusing on hyperlocal touchpoints.'

Hugh gasped. No one had ever described him in such glowing terms. At least, Hugh assumed they were glowing.

The electric, velvety resonance continued: 'Mike believes in mission-critical pain point mindsharing, value-added visibility, sustainable talent relationship management, seamless passion productivity, and delivering both quick wins and greater returns on investment in this next generation new economy. Through rightshoring, reverse fulfillment, innovative bandwidth expansion, and bizmeth process outsourcing, this best-of-breed CEO has the cadence, creative enterprise employer branding solutions and innovative co-opetition skills to get early-stage eyeballs on CGM's event horizon, free value, and innovative logistical leverage with a long tail in both local and outsourced, bricks-and-mortar and online profit centers.'

In fact, Hugh was wasn't sure what any of those things were, or even whether they made any sense. But he could tell from the voice over's tone, it was all good. Very good. This Mike Guy was someone to watch out for.

Hugh's head ached as his mind swung between wanting to ask for the guy's autograph, and wanting to punch him in the face, or even, to throw a shoe at him as soon as he appeared on stage.

But he didn't come on stage. Instead, the same photograph of Mike J. Guy from the annual report remained on screen, with 'Voice of Mike J. Guy' superimposed across the bottom with a little icon of a microphone.

An attractive woman appeared at the podium. The same one Hugh used to send out whenever he didn't feel like facing those whose money he was in charge of. Or at least, it looked like her. Hugh couldn't remember her name. They all looked the same: someone attractive enough to distract from the company's financials, and feminine enough to give the illusion of improved representation.

If there was one thing women were good for in business – well, another thing women were good for in business – it was taking the fall. Crowds were less likely to throw things at women, he'd observed, although they did get yelled at a lot more. But what was the harm in that?

Hugh stood up. 'Coward!' he shouted. 'Why don't you come out and face us?'

He went to take off one of his shoes, struggling with the laces, before Parker grabbed his arm and stopped him.

'Sit down!' he hissed.

It was just as well, really. Hugh's custom-fit Monté Stosterone alligator skin shoes had cost him a fortune. He didn't want to risk scratching them on Mike Guy's screen.

'We remind our shareholders that, while we value all of your voices, we must apply a strict code of conduct. Any further outbursts will result in the shareholder's immediate barring,' the woman at the podium said. A security guard moved towards Hugh's row of chairs and shot him a pointed look.

Hugh sat down heavily, a bolt of pain striking his core as his tailbone connected with the hard plastic seat. He stared at the woman with the microphone. Maybe it was a different woman to last year. Was she blonde? Hugh couldn't remember. If only she was wearing a skirt instead of trousers. If only she would turn slightly on an angle. Then, Hugh swore, he'd remember.

'Moving on, we begin with a report on financials over the last two quarters.'

Hugh could feel his blood boil as the report dragged on. It was even more boring than when he was in charge, and had the power to tell that little bespectacled guy to speed things up.

Picking his teeth and kicking the chair in front of him, Hugh sat through several other reports. None even mentioned the AutoAutomator system.

It was as if they wanted to completely obliterate Hugh's contributions to the company.

Finally, the woman announced it was time for shareholder input.

Hugh nearly bolted out of his seat.

'I want to know what's going on!' he shouted.

'Sir, I don't want to have to ask you again. You need to adhere to the regulations of the proceedings. There will be plenty of time for individual questions at the end of the meeting.'

Parker pulled Hugh back down again. Just because he was a bit older than the rest of the group, and because his money was a bit older too, Parker always acted like he was in charge. Hugh scowled. He'd never stuck around for shareholder questions before, but it looked as if he'd have to this time.

A man shuffled on to the stage and began to read from a list of items, his voice a low drone.

Normally, Hugh spent this time willing the gathered audience to do what they usually did. To vote halfheartedly, in line with whatever the board recommended. The vast majority of shareholders were institutional investors. Big companies invested in the firm.

Back when Hugh had first become CEO of his father's firm, around two-thirds of all investors across the market were other investment companies. Now, it was more like four-fifths.

Ostensibly, these companies were meant to vote according to the best interests of their members. Teachers and nurses saving for retirement, construction workers paying into health insurance funds. But it was a simple matter to give the CEO of a particularly large investment company a position on your board – or, if appearances of impropriety were of concern, a position on the board of one of your board member's boards – along with a generous compensation package.

That CEO, in turn, would give you a position on their board, and well, friends don't vote against other friend's pay raises, do they?

Still, there were, from time to time, a few surprises. The remaining handful of 'retail' investors – individuals and family trusts and small groups that weren't worth bribing but were far less predictable than the big institutional investors – occasionally threw up a challenge.

Hugh and his team had engineered a range of solutions to this problem. After all, that was the reason why they held the shareholder meetings on a Wednesday morning. In a city carefully selected to be located the furthest from where the majority of their retail investors lived. In a locale no one would choose for a vacation they could claim on tax.

Somewhere dreary and gray, and far from an airport was the ticket.

Of course, it was still possible to vote without actually attending the meeting, by submitting a proxy form. But only 30% of retail investors exercised their right to vote, compared with 90% of the institutional investors, making the already tiny fraction of retail investor votes even less significant.

For particularly thorny issues, where the board wasn't assured of an overwhelming majority of institutional support before the vote, they could easily persuade the few retail investors who did bother to attend with the distribution of strategically timed goody bags. Candy and free pens distracted their attention away from a particularly bad set of numbers the company was legally obligated to flash up on the screen. Or they'd give out free drink bottles or caps with the company logo during an admission of some wrongdoing.

Hugh was proud of the culture of apathy he had fostered. Though, 'apathy' wasn't quite the right word. Hugh didn't know what was.

It wasn't so much that the shareholders didn't care about the company. It was that the issues they were asked to vote on weren't the issues the shareholders cared about, and even then, they weren't convinced their vote would make any difference.

'The final issue up for vote is the CEO's compensation package.'

Hugh gripped the edges of his chair, the way he always did when it came time for a large group of people to assess his package.

Until yesterday, Hugh had been quite looking forward to this vote. And his largest windfall to date.

A couple of years ago, Pete, before he'd revealed himself to be a filthy, lying snake, had put him on to an outstanding 'compensation consultant'. Jana Dryser, who'd secured him some frankly undreamt of raises.

This year, she'd even brought in some 'talent scientist' to put together a recommendation for a simply enormous bonus and pay rise. The report he produced, filled with justifications for increasing Hugh's pay to $52 million a year, was even longer than the company's annual report.

Now that was worth the $2.4 million in consulting fees CGM had paid. Nobody could argue with that.

Jana wasn't bad looking either. No good as a wife, because then he wouldn't be able to use her services to secure future raises without violating the company's policies surrounding conflicts of interest. But Hugh wondered if he should add her to his list of prospective mistresses.

He looked around, waiting for the helpers to move through the sparse crowd and hand out the drinks and tie clips engraved with the company name he'd had Alyssa order. Something to make the suckers part with their money. Make them feel rich for a second, and they'd think rich, and thinking rich meant looking out for your own.

But today, it was Hugh's money they were discussing giving away to someone else.

'Item nine relates to the CEO's compensation,' the man droned on. Were it not for the fact that they were voting away his money, his life, Hugh might have fallen asleep. And that, Hugh knew, was by design. A boring professor type, who no one would dare question, was ideal.

Hugh himself hadn't bothered to read the voting form. He didn't care about any of the other issues, but he knew item nine off by heart. 'That the existing cap on the CEO's annual raise in compensation be removed, along with the performance conditions on the CEO's bonus'.

'I can't stand this,' Hugh choked.

'Hold on,' Parker coached. Hugh knew he must be nervous, too. The whole reason Pete had put Hugh on to Jana was because he was relying on Hugh's raise being approved, so that when it came time for his own compensation review, the average salary of comparable positions would be higher, and his own compensation would be made higher again. Which in turn would make the comps higher for Kim's review, and then Deborah's, and then finally, Parker's, in a glorious upward spiral of increasing wealth and mutual cooperation.

'Item nine proposes an increase to the CEO's salary. However, Mr. Guy has advised that he does not intend to take a salary.'

'What?!' Hugh could not contain his contempt. It exploded out of him, his bad breath visibly moving the hairpiece of the man in front of him, his eyes rolling skyward.

Lots of CEOs took salaries of $1, ostensibly to demonstrate their dedication to the company. With a negligible salary, a CEO's income was (in theory, at least) wholly reliant upon their stocks in the company increasing in value and paying dividends.

But Hugh knew the real reason that the CEOs of companies like Myriad and PearShape, and Skum Industries paid themselves token salaries. To avoid tax. And, in the case of Skum, to make people like them. After all, most of Skum's fanboys had no idea the man's billions never came from a paycheck. He got to walk around looking like some sort of volunteer worker, a billionaire philanthropist of the highest order.

That was why Hugh admired him.

Yet Hugh had never heard of a CEO taking $0 before.

This Mike J. Guy must be desperate for adoration.

But if that was the case, why hadn't he bothered to show up and bask in the admiration of the (admittedly paltry) crowd?

Perhaps this Mike J. Guy wasn't so smart after all, Hugh smirked. With no salary, officially, he wouldn't be an 'employee' of the company. And that meant losing all the other perks: company car, vacation home, assistant, health insurance, travel allowance… Hugh's smile fell and his stomach turned as he realized the extent of his own loss.

'Mr. Guy has also advised that he will not be taking compensation in the form of shareholdings. As a result, the board has recommended the shareholders not approve the item as written.'

Hugh's eyes bulged, his stomach somersaulting, the room spinning as the voting proceeded.

This Mike J. Guy wasn't content to take his position as CEO and destroy his legacy.

Along with this new board stacked with his stooges, Guy wanted to destroy the entire position of CEO. Not just at CGM, but at every company. Parker's forehead was slick with sweat in spite of the chilly air. Deborah was biting her lips, and not in a sexy way.

The voting complete, the woman returned to the podium. 'Now, we move on to shareholder-generated issues.'

Hugh shot out of his seat again. 'I have an issue!' he shouted.

The woman frowned. 'Shareholder-generated issues must be raised by the due date and via the appropriate forms. You can submit your issue for the next meeting via our website.'

The website, Hugh scoffed. The form for submitting shareholder issues was accessible only via a complicated trail of crumbs that led through page after page of CGM corporate propaganda and only worked half the time.

'Moving along,' she glanced at her notes, 'we have a proposal that the company disclose how it chooses the recipients of its annual charitable donations.'

There were seven such useless motions that needed laborious explanations and equally laborious discussion and votes before finally, it was time for questions.

Rocketing out of his seat, propelled by pure adrenaline, Hugh pushed an old man with long hair out of the way. A fat woman seated unfairly close to the microphone got there first. She began a long-winded diatribe ranging from environmental concerns to a lack of diversity in the company's managerial and leadership positions, to some frankly wild accusations about several of the subsidiaries' union-busting activities. They were all true, of course, but wild nonetheless. Hugh watched the big red numbers count down on the giant clock next to the podium. They'd brought it in a few years ago, to stop people exactly like this woman from rambling on for too long.

Hugh felt his insides shrivel. He'd encountered far too many rambling 'questions' like this, which inevitably failed to culminate in an actual question – and deftly hand-balled them to one of his PR team. All part of his 'hands off' style, Hugh used to say. 'Putting his trust in his people' – though he used the term very much in the possessive sense, and not in a manner which implied he belonged to the group of staff which actually ran the place.

But Mike J. Guy didn't do that.

'Trish, thank you for your question,' Guy's almost too-perfect voice rang out loud and clear through the speakers. 'You've raised a number of really important points – ones we will definitely take into consideration going forward. Let me assure you these issues have not gone unnoticed by myself, or the rest of the team here at CGM, and over the next fiscal year, they will be among our top priorities, as we work to further strengthen CGM's position. Your question has really highlighted some of the key items that will inform our agenda going forward over the next twelve months, and I thank you for that. There is no opinion we value more at CGM than the voices of our shareholders.'

To Hugh's immense surprise, the woman returned to her seat, rather than booing or throwing anything. In fact, she looked downright pleased, nodding to the even fatter man sitting next to her.

Hugh grabbed the microphone. 'This is a sham!' he shouted, the microphone squealing in horror as his spittle contacted the grille.

'Sir, please identify yourself to the CEO and the rest of the board.'

'I am the CEO!' Hugh roared. 'I am Hugh J. Richardson, CEO of

CGM.'

'No you aren't,' the fat woman retorted. 'It says right here, Mike J. Guy, CEO.' She jabbed a finger at the fraud's photo in the annual report. Hugh noticed that she'd drawn a love heart around his head.

'Yeah,' her companion piped up. 'If you're the CEO, why's he up there instead of you?'

'He's not up there!' Hugh cried, 'It's just a screen!'

'I've been to these meetings for the last four years,' the man Hugh had pushed interjected. He breathed a sigh of relief. Finally, someone had recognized him! Finally, someone was coming to his defense. 'It's always just a guy on a screen,' he finished.

'That guy was me!' Hugh cried.

The man squinted at Hugh, sweeping the greasy tendrils of his hair away from his eyes, then looked back at the screen. 'You look a bit like him, I'll give you that,' he said. 'But he's much better looking.'

'You think I don't know that?' Hugh shook his head. 'That's beside the point. The point is–'

'I'm sorry sir, your time is up. Please return to your seat and we'll move on to the next questioner.'

Hugh stared at the big red timer flashing '0:00'.

'You don't understand,' Hugh protested. 'I am the CEO! Don't you remember my face? My name?'

'What did you say your name was again?' the fat woman asked.

'Hugh! Hugh J. Richardson!'

Someone behind him laughed. 'That doesn't sound like a CEO's name!'

He was wrong. Hugh knew that his name sounded exactly like a CEO's name – and not just because he was a CEO and that was his name. Rather, Hugh knew that 'Hugh J. Richardson' sounded like a CEO's name because the company had shelled out thousands to an onomastics expert to determine what his name should be.

Like the company, Hugh's own family had undergone so many high-level mergers he had a plethora of surnames-as-middle names to choose from. Fifty grand, the guy got, just for suggesting Hugh select 'J'.

It was, he blistered, the same middle initial as Mike J. Guy.

'Security!'

Two guards gripped Hugh by the shoulders and frog-marched him away from the microphone and towards the door.

'I'm the CEO!' he protested to the one who had given him trouble at the entrance, feebly attempting to wave the rolled up annual report. 'Don't you recognize me?' he begged the other.

Hugh had always taken great pride in his 'hands off' approach. He'd described hands-off-ed-ness as the sole pillar of his managerial approach when he'd been interviewed for Top CEO Magazine's special on the 1000 Most Important CEOs.

He'd planned a whole chapter on hands-off-ed-ness, before his editor ruined everything.

But now, Hugh regretted this approach.

How he wished he'd gotten to know his employees.

Learned a few of their names.

He shook that thought from his head. CGM had thousands of employees. Or hundreds. Hugh wasn't sure which. But he could have shown his face more often than once a year. Made sure they knew his name.

Perhaps then, the woman running the proceedings, or even the security guards, might have recognized him. Might not have thrown him out.

At the very least, Hugh thought, as he lay bruised on the pavement outside, they might not have thrown him so hard.

Then again, he mused, CGM probably outsourced their security in any case.

For a fleeting moment, Hugh's heart leapt as he felt the cardboard teeth of a faux chainsaw against his leg. At last, someone had recognized him!

But then he realized, they would have attacked anyone in a suit.

As he looked up from the pavement, attempting to kick the protester away and straighten his tie simultaneously, it was Hugh's turn to recognize someone.

Maddy.

She'd caught the whole thing on camera.

CHAPTER 5

Bruised in both ego and backside, Hugh rounded the corner to the bar where Pete was waiting.

'Is it because of my drinking?' Hugh confronted Pete as the bartender prepared his drink.

Pete actually laughed. 'If we started throwing people under the bus for that, we'd all be locked up in rehab within the week!'

Pete was right. Hugh had read somewhere that high-income individuals drank more than any other group. They were all having five-martini lunches, hiding whisky in their bureaus, sealing deals with a handshake and a clink.

They had to stick together. They always did.

Even if Pete was a lying, disloyal snake.

A couple of years ago, when he'd introduced sweeping drug and alcohol tests across CGM, Hugh and the board had ensured that C-suite execs would be exempt. It was obscene – the idea of Hugh and the other high-ups holed up in their executive bathrooms, urinating into a jar or whatever you had to do.

A few executives Hugh knew had really gone off the rails. He'd even attended some of their interventions – they always had the best drinks.

Like anything in corporate life, there were whole companies that specialized in interventions. Facilitating expensive parties for board members to confront their wayward CEOs.

'Somebody's gotta live the dream!' Pete continued, raising his glass.

A sense of relief flowed through Hugh's body along with the whisky. Pete was, as always, right.

They worked hard. They deserved a few drinks. The occasional high, or office dalliance. Why else did they have private bathrooms?

Actually, that reminded Hugh of an article he'd read in the Hardly Business Review. Or rather, a headline from HBR that he'd glanced at, but not tapped on. Some top CEO was not-quite-mandating but strongly suggesting the use of 'smart pills' to boost performance. Hugh wanted to ask Parker whether their drug tests were sensitive enough to distinguish between different types of drugs, so they could keep their employees on the right ones. Not that Parker would know. He was hopeless when it came to anything medical or scientific. But he'd know who to demand an answer from.

Hugh's phone vibrated. Speak of the devil.

But Parker wasn't saying anything.

There was just a strange noise, alternating between heavy breathing and a high-pitched whine.

'Are you okay? Have you been kidnapped? Where are you?'

'I just stepped outside of the meeting. Hugh - it's happened to me,' Parker whispered, his voice cracking. 'It's happened to me!'

'What has?'

'I got my assistant to send through the report for our annual meeting. I thought it was a bit strange I hadn't seen it yet, but as you know, our meeting's not until well after CGM's, so I didn't think too much of it,' Parker's words tumbled out of the phone. 'Anyway, Cherry sent it through, and I clicked on that little magnifying glass thingy and looked for my name – I'm not in there.'

'Calm down,' Hugh coached. 'Maybe the search function's broken.' Computers always had it in for Hugh. Maybe they hated Parker, too.

'It isn't. I looked for the CEO's letter, and I found it. Just like yours – but with slightly different words – and there was his name and photo at the bottom. John K. Nelson. Who the hell is that?'

Hugh frowned. 'Never heard of him.' How had these nobodies gotten their jobs? Everyone knew it wasn't what but who you knew that counted, and until today, no one had ever heard of Mike J. Guy or John K. Nelson.

'Parker's been replaced too.'

Pete's face turned gray. 'I have to call my assistant.'

As Pete stood up from his chair, the bar's double doors burst open, like some scene from an old movie. There was the rest of the gang. And Deborah, of course.

'You didn't miss much,' Kim assured Hugh, signaling for the bartender to pull down the entire contents of his top shelf.

'Did they mention me at all?'

'Not even once.'

'Or any of my projects? Like the AutoAutomator project, or-' Hugh struggled to think of anything else he'd achieved over the past financial year. Still, the AutoAutomator project should have been more than enough. Kira had promised it would save the company at least $35 million a year in labor costs, or they'd refund CGM in full.

And what a refund that would be. The AutoAutomator software was the single most expensive purchase Hugh had ever signed off on – with a nice kickback for himself, of course. But the results sounded so good, Hugh had been enamored from the very beginning. It was genius.

Why just automate when you could automate automation?

It wasn't only Hugh. The whole board was enraptured. Every last one of them had adopted AutoAutomator in their own companies – Hugh picking up little referral bonuses along the way.

Plus, the fact that everyone else was doing it made it a sure bet. More than that, it meant anyone who didn't would be behind the curve.

A hot flash seared through Hugh's body.

What if the AutoAutomator hadn't worked?

That would explain why they hadn't mentioned it at the annual meeting.

Why he'd lost his job.

Hugh grabbed his copy of the annual report from the bar, now torn from his time on the pavement and sodden with spilled whisky. He flicked through to the page that compared the company's number of workers to last year's.

There was no change. Well, no real change. Not the sort of dramatic change required to make the dramatic savings the AutoAutomator people had promised. Even if the software had only automated or outsourced away the jobs of CGM's highest-paid analysts, there should have been at least 500 jobs gone – and Hugh didn't think they had that many analysts. Besides, surely you wouldn't work from the top-down.

The jobs in most danger of outsourcing and automating were things like cleaning or typing – basic jobs that brought in basic wages. Hugh struggled to think of how many of those jobs would have to be cut for the AutoAutomator to make the necessary savings. Surely it would be in the thousands.

He almost wished he'd done these calculations beforehand, checked the feasibility of their guarantee. It had sounded too good to be true for a reason.

The software had failed.

'Don't worry about it!' Kira had said. 'Just let it run in the background. You do your job, and let the AutoAutomator do its job!'

Hugh had always wanted to make a mark, other than the mark he made when the family investment firm went under during his tenure as CEO, and he supposed this was it. Though it wasn't at all what he'd imagined.

Pete returned to the bar, almost missing the stool as he sat down. He looked even paler than when he'd left.

'I'm not there,' he said, his voice barely a whisper. 'I've been erased.'

The bar exploded into a chaos of beeps and shouts as the other CEOs called their respective assistants.

'Dammit!' Kim shouted, stabbing at his phone. 'What's my damn code? Let me in!'

Hugh's eyes remained glued to the report, burning as he stared at the employee figures.

He'd never spent so long looking at them, and the more he looked, the more the numbers seemed to jump around and come alive before his eyes.

'What are you staring at?' Parker asked, signaling for another drink.

'I think I know why we've been replaced,' Hugh said.

He didn't want to say what had to come next.

His tongue, his teeth, his lips, didn't want to form the words that said it was all his fault. Of course, had he been claiming responsibility for something good, the words would have rolled right out of his mouth. But right now, he had to admit responsibility for something very bad indeed.

'I think the software failed.'

'What software?'

'The AutoAutomator software. Look,' Hugh pointed at the table where CGM's current year-end employment figures were printed next to last year's. 'Notice any difference?'

'They're practically the same.'

'Exactly. We should have seen massive layoffs in order to get the kinds of savings Kira promised.'

'But there's nothing.'

'Exactly.'

Parker gulped down his drink. 'No wonder.' He refilled again. 'Can't we do something though? Wasn't there some guarantee?'

Hugh nodded. 'A minimum savings clause in the contract. If the company doesn't save at least that amount, we'll get a full refund.'

'Surely if we recoup the money we poured into this, we'll get a second chance? Somewhere would hire us.' He cast a look at Kim, who was still trying to unlock his phone. Kim presided over the disappearance of $30 billion of market capitalization, in part due to an acquisition he'd made which cost the company he ran before PearShape, HQP, over $8.8 billion. And still, he'd walked away with

$13 million that year, including a 'performance bonus' of $2.4 million! That was the point, after all, of stacking the board with as many friends as possible.

But could it really be the case that Hugh's mistake had cost more than Kim's?

And if the entire board had been replaced, then exactly who had replaced them? The shareholders? It was possible in theory. Had an extraordinary meeting been called, there was every chance Hugh had ignored the notification. The word 'meeting' made his eyes glaze over.

'I'm out too.' Kim looked terrified – and with good reason, Hugh supposed. He might have been able to weather one very public screw up, but two? Especially now that his number of friends on boards were dropping like flies.

'Me too,' Deborah said.

Hugh breathed a sigh of relief. If this could happen to Deb, who, he grudgingly admitted, worked harder than the rest of the board, then it could happen to any of them. It wasn't only him.

Though it was only a matter of time before the others remembered who it was who had recommended Kira and her defective AutoAutomator software in the first place.

Hugh had to do what he did best: deflect attention before anyone cottoned on.

'Let's go get our refunds.'

CHAPTER 6

Hugh rode in Parker's car. He didn't feel like being near Pete. Or even what counted as 'near' in Pete's twelve-seater limo. Besides, as the CEO of PharmaX, Parker's car had the most extensive collection of drinks.

Speaking of which, Hugh thought as he helped himself to another glass, he almost wished it was his drinking that was the reason for his fall from grace. He'd rather it be a personal failure than a business failure. A personal failure, Maddy could probably squeeze a good story out of for his autobiography. Hell, it might even sell on its own if he screwed up enough.

A horrible thought struck Hugh – would the publisher even want his book after this?

He'd been a fool. Sucked in by that smooth-talking Kira with all her promises of kickbacks and bonuses. And the savings for the company. But then, Hugh wasn't the only one. Even Kim, CEO of one of the biggest tech companies in the world, had been right behind the decision. Though sometimes, Hugh suspected Kim didn't know all that much about computers. After all, he'd asked Hugh's son for help clearing his browser history.

'How can they do this?' Hugh fumed, sloshing gin over his tie. He'd really had too many drinks now. So many, in fact, he'd had to take off his jacket, as it was now soaking in $800-a-bottle liquor. 'There are proshedursh!'

'What gets me,' Parker said, also a little too loudly as the car swung into the parking lot, 'is that none of us knew! And nobody seems to know! None of our asshistants said anything. Cherry seemed genuinely surprised when she read out the CEO's letter from the report. And let me tell you, she's not that good an actress!'

Hugh and Parker knew what he meant – in the bedroom. Or more likely, the boardroom, where Parker carried out most of his affairs. But the news of his sudden demotion must have shaken him, for Parker to mess up his innuendo so badly as to imply he was anything less than brimming with sexual prowess. Acting as the face of a company best known for its little blue pills had made Parker sensitive about these things.

'Gentlemen, welcome!' some little man was at the ground floor, ready to greet them.

'Don't you welcome us!' Parker shook his fist.

'Please, come in. The rest of your party are upstairs. We've prepared some snacks and drinks-' He looked at, and perhaps, Hugh speculated, smelled him, 'coffee,' he continued. 'Lots of coffee.'

The small start-up that made AutoAutomator had offices on the tenth floor. Their boardroom wasn't as quirky as the meeting facilities at PearShape, where Kim insisted everyone sit on bouncy balls or swing in mini hammocks while robots served them some sort of foul-tasting green juice. At least while the cameras were around. But neither was it the stuffy, wood-panelled halls of Hardings Bank and Investment, where everything was leather-upholstered mahogany.

In fact, Boardroom A, where the others were already seated, was typical of most meeting rooms Hugh spent time in. Shiny walls. Shiny table. High-backed chairs, with a variety of knobs and levers that intimidated him. In fact, they were the exact same ergonomic chairs they'd gotten at CGM a few years back.

The first time Hugh had tried operating one of them, he'd somehow managed to plummet almost to the floor, narrowly avoiding grazing his chin on the oval desk. Attempting to remedy the situation before anyone noticed, he twisted a different knob which tilted the seat portion of the chair so far forward he almost slid off.

Unable to rectify matters no matter how he tried to (discreetly) fiddle with the knobs and levers, Hugh maintained this uncomfortable pose for the entire meeting, claiming afterwards, when Pete had the gall to offer him a tutorial in the chair's operation, that he'd read that a lowered sitting position and forward angle were good for improving posture, dynamic thinking, and boosted analytical skills by 15%. Since that sounded like exactly the sort of garbage they'd print in Top CEO Magazine, Pete had let it slip. Every meeting since, he'd had Alyssa set up his chair beforehand.

Of course, Alyssa wasn't here today.

Sitting down carefully, Hugh watched as Pete headed straight for the mini donuts at the end of the table. The bastard got his donut after all.

'Where is Kira?' Hugh demanded.

'Kira is part of our marketing team. My name is Jai – the lead programmer of the AutoAutomator software.'

'So she's a coward? Doesn't want to face us?' Hugh could almost feel his face changing color.

'It's actually pretty typical for these tech firms,' Deborah said. 'Their products are sold by women, and even predominantly used by women in a lot of cases, but the ones making decisions about how they are programmed tend to be men.'

Hugh scowled. He didn't need Deb explaining things to him. That was the worst thing about hiring someone simply because they were a woman. They were always playing the woman card.

'So,' Jai joined them at the table, taking a seat in front of a shiny laptop. 'I got the impression you have some concerns about the AutoAutomator software? We always anticipate a few teething issues in the initial stages of any roll-out.'

Kim nodded. At least, Hugh thought he saw Kim nod. The man's face was practically buried in a freshly mixed choc-pear-spinach smoothie. It reminded Hugh of nothing so much as the raw sewerage he'd unfortunately witnessed at Freshwater Streams.

'What seems to be the problem?'

'The program doesn't work!' Parker shouted before spotting a plate of maguro.

'It hasn't affected the figures at all!' Hugh yelled. Someone appeared at his side with a silver tray containing a pile of those little pastries with the almonds and raisins. Hugh took one. Then, realizing he had plenty of room in his jacket pocket, he took another.

'Hmm,' Jai, to his credit, looked puzzled. 'Let me pull up your numbers.'

After a few taps and swipes, during which Hugh helped himself to a third pastry, Jai projected CGM's numbers on the wall.

'Everything looks good to me,' Jai said. ' In fact, the AutoAutomator appears to be performing even better than we anticipated. Look at the savings - $38 million already, and projected ongoing savings of $52 million annually.'

The numbers sounded vaguely familiar, but for the moment, his mouth full of flaky, buttery pastry, Hugh couldn't remember why he'd been agitated in the first place.

'Those figures are bullshit!' Parker shouted.

'You think there's some mistake? Let me bring up PharmaX.'

Once again, the screen glowed green with enormous realized and projected savings.

'This is garbage!' Kim chipped in. 'What about the others?'

Jai went through each of their companies, and every dashboard glowed green.

'The software certainly seems to be working,' he enthused. 'Risk is down, profits are up. Public perception is up, operating expenses have fallen and are predicted to fall further in the coming year. Employee satisfaction is improving, legal expenses have decreased… and the stock price is climbing as we speak!' Jai smiled. 'Gentlemen, it looks like you have nothing to worry about!'

'Look at the employee figures,' Deborah demanded.

Jai clicked around. Just as their own reports had shown, none of the companies' employee numbers had changed substantially, either in terms of the total number of employees, or the proportions of on- and off-shore workers.

PharmaX and PearShape had even increased their workforces.

'Now, you tell me,' Parker said, spilling his coffee, 'How have these supposed enormous savings been delivered without affecting employment figures? The whole point of this software was to outsource and automate the work of our least productive employees, wasn't it?'

Jai frowned. 'You're right. Let me check the output. There should be a summary of all the positions which have been outsourced or automated since the program's roll-out. Just a moment – I'll amalgamate your reports'.

Hugh leaned back in his chair – cautiously. As he waited for the report to run he scoffed another of those little pastries.

'Here we are! It seems the AutoAutomator has indeed identified candidates whose pay was not justified by their contribution to the bottom line. Each of your companies has saved between fifteen and five hundred million so far.'

'Excellent!' Deborah enthused as she popped a truffle into her mouth.

Whether it was the good news, or the comfortable chair, Hugh felt his shoulders relax a little. The software had worked. Once he showed the key shareholders the enormous savings he'd made, he was sure they'd give him his job back, and Mike J. Guy would be toast.

'Here we are,' Jai said. He scrolled down to the first line. 'This employee earned more than four times what industry analysts' figures say they should have.'

'Disgusting!' Parker chimed in again.

'And another, who earned nine times that figure!'

'Obscene!'

Hugh felt his stomach tighten. Perhaps he was still hungry. Where were those pastries?

'In fact,' Jai continued, 'this group of employees has seen their salaries grow at a rate of fifty-eight times the rate of other employees.'

'Who are they? What departments?'

Hugh's stomach tightened again.

Jai clicked the bar at the bottom of the screen, and scrolled across to the employee name and ID columns. He swallowed.

'Pete S. Harding, Kim W. Park, Parker L. Jefferson, Deborah Frost, and Hugh J. Richardson.'

'Bastards!' Parker yelled, sloshing the coffee down his tie.

'He's talking about us, you numbskull!'

'The software was supposed to outsource employees!' Pete exploded.

'Technically, you are employees,' Jai said in a voice little more than a twitter. 'Or rather, were.'

'Still, it wasn't supposed to outsource us!' Deborah cried.

Jai tapped away at his computer, each keystroke assaulting Hugh's ears.

'Actually, your jobs haven't been outsourced,' he said.

Hugh breathed a sigh of relief. It was all just a big misunderstanding.

'They've been automated.'

CHAPTER 7

'You're telling me this Mike J. Guy isn't even real?'

Hugh felt a pang of regret – if Mike J. Guy wasn't real, he wouldn't be able to punch him in the face.

'That's right,' Jai said slowly. 'As you no doubt remember, the primary aim of the AutoAutomator is to analyze your - sorry, a workforce, and then, on the basis of our proprietary algorithms, identify positions which can be both profitably and beneficially automated or outsourced, and to then automatically automate or outsource them.'

'We know that!' Hugh fumed. It was Lila, with her colored hair and her union badges, who had insisted they insert that damn 'beneficial' clause . No doubt this was all her fault.

The unions had too much power. If the software had been able to focus on profit, maybe it would have done its job properly, and Hugh could have kept his.

'It was agreed,' Jai flashed a copy of the contract on the screen, as though it were a shield, 'that those positions which showed the most potential for improvement in both profit and benefit to the company would be automated or outsourced first. Here, let me show you a graph of your salaries relative to other employees.'

The screen changed to show a whole lot of blank space on the left-hand side, and then, on the far right, the plotted salaries of Hugh and his fellow CEOs.

Hugh felt sick as he saw how his column measured up to – or failed to measure up to – the columns of the other CEOs.

His was even smaller than Deborah's.

'No wonder this damn software doesn't work,' Parker snorted. His name, of course, was at the top of the chart. 'Your graph's broken! It doesn't even display the other employees' incomes.'

Jai frowned. Then, he started to zoom in.

At 400% zoom, there was still nothing.

At 1,000% zoom, the computer refused to go any further. But Hugh thought he could just begin to detect a faint blue line at the bottom of the screen.

'There,' Jai said. 'It's not broken. That long tail represents the rest of employees' incomes, relative to your own.'

'Fine, I accept we're in the firing line as far as income goes,' Deborah said. 'But that doesn't explain why we've lost our board positions at each others' companies as well.

'We only receive a small amount of compensation for those roles,' Kim nodded. 'A token!'

Now, Jai brought up a list of those 'tokens '.

$200,000 per board member at CGM.

$250,000 at ToyStar.

$950,000 at PearShape.

PharmaX was the most generous, at $2.17 million per board member.

'Even the smallest 'token' amount of compensation you receive is routinely double what other highly-paid employees earn, and around four times as much as your average employees earn. In a year.'

'Okay, we get paid a lot,' Pete protested. 'So what? You can't just bring in any old person to perform our jobs!'

'And you certainly can't bring in a machine to replace us!' Parker slurred.

Jai didn't say anything. He didn't need to. The fact was, a machine had been brought in to replace each and every one of them, and nobody had noticed. No one had noticed they'd been made redundant, not even the CEOs themselves.

And nobody had noticed their replacements weren't human – again, not even the CEOs themselves.

Jai cleared his throat. 'Perhaps I can explain a little how it works.'

'Please,' said Hugh, his voice even colder than the room.

'The AutoAutomator has three key functions: analysis, outsourcing, and automation. When the software is installed at any given company, it performs an initial analysis, identifying the roles which, if outsourced or automated, would provide the greatest return and highest benefit to the company.'

'We know all that! Get to the point!' Parker demanded.

'Once these positions have been identified, the AutoAutomator will, from its constantly-updating database of global employment networks, offshore factories and mechanical turks, outsource the relevant positions.'

Hugh could now vaguely remember some of this stuff from the presentations Kira and her colleagues had given before they signed the contracts. He'd paid more attention to the part where Kira had explained the structure through which he'd be compensated for each referral he made. After all, none of this side of things would ever affect him.

'In the case that automation is required, the AutoAutomator will, in the case of physical tasks, like building a car or laying bricks, search its network of robotics and mechatronics experts, initiate a tender process.'

'So you've replaced us with robots?'

'I haven't replaced you with anyone – or anything,' Jai corrected. 'It's all the AutoAutomator.'

This, Hugh now remembered, was exactly what he'd planned to say to any employees – or rather, former employees who complained to the media. What he'd intended to say to Lila, if she started bringing in lawyers and reporters. That he, Hugh, had not replaced anyone. It was all the AutoAutomator.

'And no,' Jai continued. 'No robots in this case. Social functions, like customer facing roles, or cerebral functions, like data analysis – are automated via software. The AutoAutomator's patented artificial intelligence utilizes machine learning to automate tasks with no or limited physical components.'

'What does all that technobabble mean?' Kim demanded. Hugh had never seen him so rattled. Usually Kim at least made some attempt to pretend to understand what programmers said.

'Essentially, the AutoAutomator, in performing its analysis of the roles within a company, amasses a vast amount of information, which it stores in a database. Once a decision has been made to automate a position electronically the AutoAutomator simply generates a script, in your case, called AutoCEO, based on the information in the database to perform the duties associated with that role.'

'You think a spreadsheet can make up for the collective wisdom of this room?' Parker gestured angrily around the table.

'Of course not. The AutoCEO's database is made up not only of all the decisions made by yourselves, but all your predecessors, as far back as records go. Think of it as the collective wisdom of your company's entire life. And every other company's life. Including all the failed ones.'

'Ha!' Kim looked as if he were about to make a point that might save them. Hugh leaned forward in his seat, careful not to touch any knobs. 'Why would you want to add in the decisions of failed boards and CEOs?'

'So that AutoCEO knows what *not* to do. In fact,' Jai clicked around a bit more, 'I can show you a visualization of the model AutoCEO is currently running.'

Different sized pies filled the screen, each representing an individual company. Inside each were even more circles, colored red and green.

'The size of each circle indicates the weight the system will give to each company's past decisions,' Jai explained. 'Green indicates a cluster or series of decisions the software has identified as worthy of replication, should similar conditions arise again.'

'And red?' Deborah asked.

'Those would be decisions the software has identified as leading to failure and losses. AutoCEO must be trained on both positive and negative outcomes.'

Hugh watched as Dan's face turned as red as the circle for HQP, the company he ran before PearShape, which filled close to a quarter of the enormous screen.

'But where did you get this data?' Parker raged.

'A lot of it is publicly available,' Jai said. 'The data in your annual reports. The financials you file each quarter. Your interviews in magazines.'

Hugh gulped as he thought of how proud he'd been to be included in the 1000 Most Important CEOs. He'd never imagined his polished comments about shining your shoes and enhancing your personal brand would be mined and used to replace him.

'That represents only a tiny fraction of what we do,' Deborah objected.

'Besides -' Hugh began. He wished he had one of the writers he outsourced his reports to here to help him express what he needed to say in a way that didn't leave him open to litigation. 'The content of those reports has been, how shall we say, "massaged" to show our companies in the best possible light.'

Jai smiled. 'Rest assured, the software takes all that into consideration. As I was saying, a lot of the data is publicly available. But the rest of the data comes from your memos, emails, internal reports. Anything electronic, AutoAutomator has analyzed it and built the results into the AutoCEO model.'

'How- how is that legal? We never signed up for that!'

Jai returned to the contract. 'Actually, you gave AutoAutomator unrestricted access to any and all data from your servers that we need in the provision of our services.'

Here, at last, was Hugh's silver lining.

'But I hardly use my work email!'

Hugh carried out most of his communication via private accounts – in direct contravention of company policy. Still, when you were CEO, who was going to stop you? It wasn't as if Hugh was going to lose his job for forwarding a few commercial-in-confidence documents to Pete from his big_richardson6969 account.

Jai cleared his throat. 'During our initial testing phases, we realized that a significant proportion of top-level decisions were being made via personal correspondence. But the software has access to that data, too.'

Hugh looked down at the half-eaten pastry in his hand. No wonder they knew what he liked. They knew everything about him. All his secrets. Many of which were a good deal less savory than this pastry.

'But how?' Pete spluttered.

'We have access to any data which passes through our servers. It's in the contract. Right underneath the clause describing your referral bonuses.'

'Referral bonuses?' Deborah spluttered.

'Sure. Every CEO who recommends the software to another company receives a bonus when they sign on. I'm sure Kira went over this with you,' Jai looked puzzled.

'That's why you recommended this software?' Parker shouted at Hugh.

'So you've been – what do you call it,' Kim flapped his hands about as if he were physically rather than just verbally stuck in place. 'Routing our data through your servers? Surely that's illegal!'

It was, Hugh recalled vaguely. In fact, Kim's own company had been in trouble for exactly that – intercepting user data and running it through their servers, stripping out all the useful personal details and selling them to third parties. Mostly advertisers. But a handful of sexual predators and identity thieves, too.

'Actually, we run all your servers. Or rather, you use our servers.'

'Ha!' Kim exclaimed. 'That's not true! Our data isn't on servers! It's in the cloud!'

This, Hugh mused, was why they needed Kim on the team. His previous reservations about Kim's technological skills evaporated. When they really needed him, Kim could pull out the big guns and sling around techno mumbo jumbo like the best of them.

Jai coughed. 'The cloud is just a network of servers,' he explained.

'So you have all our private data – and all our staff's private data too?' Hugh bet there'd be some juicy stuff.

'Not exactly,' Jai pulled up the figures. 'It would appear that the junior staff at your companies do not engage in much personal communication via company devices.'

A hot flush swept through Hugh as he remembered the bans prohibiting staff from using anything other than corporate-approved software on their machines. He didn't know how the tech guys managed it, but it was brilliant. At least, he'd thought so at the time.

'The average age of your workers is what, thirty?' Jai continued. 'Thirty-five?'

Deborah snorted, then changed expressions as if she'd thought the better of it. She had a most unattractive snort, Hugh mused. It wasn't surprising, given the unattractive nose it came out of.

She was one of those women you could tell came from old money. Big money. Enough that she could rise to the top with a nose like that. Sure, she had enough money to do something about it – with the flick of her checkbook, Deborah could have the nation's top surgeons all vying for the chance to sculpt that misshapen lump of clay into something beautiful – or at least, passable. Smaller. More feminine. But she didn't. Why? Because she didn't have to. She was almost like a man in that way, Hugh thought.

'Our data shows that the average age of a board member is about sixty-three, sixty-four. Retirement age for most people. I suspect that might be one reason your boards were targeted by the algorithm.'

At last, Hugh thought he might see a glimmer of opportunity, but Parker beat him to it. 'That's ageism!'

Hugh wasn't exactly sure how old Parker was, but he would have pegged him around 75. It was hard to tell. Parker's reliance on PharmaX pharmaceuticals could have either prematurely aged him, or be keeping him more youthful than he ought to seem.

In any case, Hugh couldn't wait to get out of the room. He was cold, his stomach hurt – possibly from eating too many of those pastries – and he could feel the eyes of the others burning into him, even when he turned his back to them. They all knew now. It was all his fault.

'I've heard enough!' Hugh said, sniveling the fancy chair away from the table, and bumping one of its levers against Pete's leg, causing the back support to recline so far back, it aligned with the seat. As Pete cried out in pain, Hugh stood up, dusting the fallen flakes of pastry from his suit.

'I'm calling my lawyer!'

The last time Hugh had told William Marshall, attorney at law he needed help, it had been for his divorce. Marshall had offered to refer him to a specialist, but it was much cheaper for him to use Marshall and charge it to the company as a business expense. After all, Hugh's business was the company's business, he reasoned.

'Send over the contracts,' Marshall said, 'Then come see me on Friday. Don't worry. We'll get this thing solved.'

Hugh was confident they would. Not only had Marshall managed to settle the harassment suit Alyssa brought against him for a very reasonable sum, but he'd managed to squash two others that cropped up in the process. And the experts he arranged for Hugh's divorce case did such a good job, by the time the dust was settled, Bambi practically had to pay *him*.

CHAPTER 8

Hugh admired the opulent meeting room at Marshall, Marshall and Williamson. His father had taught him long ago never to trust a lawyer whose offices weren't at least three times as nice as your own.

Not that Hugh had an office of his own anymore, he supposed.

The thought made him feel sick.

It wasn't that he spent much time in the office – he didn't. But the thought of someone else sitting in his chair, using his desk, looking at his view, was abhorrent.

Hugh J. Richardson Senior's reasoning still held, though. A firm with a meeting room like this was a firm which charged its clients a lot. And a firm which could afford to charge its clients a lot was a firm whose clients won.

He tried to take some solace in this thought as he waited, alone. Hugh hadn't spoken to Pete in days. And none of the others were answering his calls.

'Hugh,' Marshall swept into the room in his characteristic cloud of expensive aftershave. 'Let's get started.'

'We can start by suing the pants off Mike J. Guy!'

Marshall frowned. 'Unless I've misunderstood what you're telling me… Mike J. Guy is not a real person.'

'So what?'

'Well, you can't bring legal action against a computer program.'

Hugh felt sick. He couldn't count the number of times he'd had legal action brought against him. Even Marshall had probably lost count. This was just one more way in which Mike J. Guy was better than him.

'You can, however, against the makers of the program.'

'Yes!' Hugh shouted, 'Sue those AutoAutomator bastards for discrimination!'

'I'm not certain that is the best angle either,' Marshall's frown deepened.

Hugh jolted. He'd never heard Marshall say something couldn't be done. Even when he'd brought his horribly messy divorce case to Marshall, he'd fixed Hugh up with an expert team right away.

'Let's say you take that path, and succeed – which is highly unlikely. It would only leave you open to discrimination suits in future. In order to show the algorithm discriminated against you because of the disproportionately older, maler, whiter makeup of your boards, you'd first have to admit that you have not been hiring in an equitable manner. Besides, from the information you've sent over, I see no evidence the algorithm targeted you on any of these demographic grounds.'

'What do you suggest then?' Hugh asked, desperate for Marshall to throw him a lifeline.

'Looking over your contract, it all comes down to two things. Unless AutoAutomator can demonstrate that automating your positions was both profitable and beneficial for the company, we can show that the software failed to perform as contracted'. Here, Marshall stubbed his finger against the contract lying on the table.

'That's what I'm saying!' Hugh exploded. 'Our experience, our wisdom, is our greatest asset! How could our companies have possibly benefited from losing our collective expertise? That's why you hire experienced CEOs and board members. To benefit from their years of experience.'

Marshall's frown deepened. 'I'm not sure you realize what you're up against.'

'Ha!' Hugh couldn't help but laugh. 'I know exactly who I'm up against. Mike J. Guy. A "man" who was literally born yesterday!' Even without the air quotes, Hugh's voice was thick with sarcasm. To be honest, he wasn't completely sure when Mike J. Guy had come on the scene, since nobody had noticed when the transition occurred. Still, 'born yesterday' was a nice rhetorical flourish, he thought.

Marshall shook his head. 'This "Mike J. Guy" has been trained with the collective wisdom – and yes, failures – of all of you. And all of the other CEOs who have signed on with AutoAutomator, or whose key decisions have been made public. We don't have to prove that you're better than a fresh face. We have to convince a court that it would be in the best interests of the company to settle for a CEO with a few decades of experience, when they could have one with the collective experience of literally thousands of CEOs.'

Hugh felt as if he could hear the cars whizzing around outside, even though they were fifty stories below. Then, he realized, it was the sound of his own blood rushing around his head.

'Essentially, the "profitable and beneficial" clause means we need to prove that you contribute to the company's bottom line. That you are worth it.'

Hugh sighed in relief. If there was one thing he knew, it was how much he was worth.

Right down to the last cent.

'It's not like we even earn as much as we used to,' Hugh grumbled. 'Look!' he thrust an article covered in graphs across the table. "CEO pay declined sharply after the latest market crash,"' he quoted, leaning back in his chair while Marshall examined the smoking gun.

Marshall frowned. 'It looks like your individual salaries have indeed declined.'

'Exactly,' Hugh beamed.

'But they've bounced back since.'

'Well, so have profits!'

'But your employees' salaries haven't.'

Hugh squirmed. 'You're a lawyer. Surely you can spin it. A drop is a drop.'

Marshall's frown deepened. 'It looks like the bulk of the change was due to the drop in the value of CGM's stocks.'

'So?'

'Well, some might say you were responsible for the share price.'

Hugh looked scandalized. 'That's not fair!'

'Let me stop you right there,' Marshall held up a hand. 'We have to demonstrate that you *are* responsible for the company.'

Perhaps Marshall was losing the plot. Hugh had spent his entire working life trying to avoid responsibility. Especially for losses. If Marshall didn't know even these basics of business, the rest of his advice was dubious too.

'Okay then,' Hugh said slowly. 'Can't you frame it that I took a pay cut when the market was doing badly? Surely that's worth something.'

'According to this chart, you didn't. Not really. Your pay remained stable, or in two cases, actually went up, during the last three crises. It was the loss in stock price that made your overall compensation package go down.'

'Regardless of where our compensation comes from,' Hugh huffed, 'we were hurting.'

Marshall frowned again. 'I'm afraid that's not how a jury will see it. Where your pay comes from does matter. The optics are bad. Don't you think your employees were hurting? CGM laid off fifteen percent of its staff, cut the pay of a further twenty, and froze the wages of everyone else. And that was before the implementation of the AutoAutomator software!'

Hugh's mouth flapped a few times, his tongue dry.

'Our ability to make tough decisions like that is precisely why we are so valuable to our companies!'

'Right,' Marshall said, looking down at his paper. 'I see the board were all awarded performance bonuses for making that decision.'

'Of course. We were protecting shareholder value.'

'Don't you think your shareholders were hurting? They trusted CGM, and by extension, its CEO and board, with their savings. It's not just the fact that, in real terms, none of you took a pay cut when the rest of the country were losing their income. Or that you used the opportunity to pause dividends, cutting off the incomes of your investors, too, without reinvestment. It's the fact that you gave yourself raises! If you enter a chart like this into evidence, you'll have no hope of winning. And you'd better pray that the other side doesn't bring it up. It's going to be tough enough to get a jury of ordinary workers to vote with you.'

Hugh grabbed the edge of the lacquered table. He could feel his fingers sticking to the wood, glued by his sweat. His heart beating in his temple. His entire world slipping away. Not because any of what Marshall was saying was news to him – he'd already anticipated all of these arguments. That's why he'd come to Marshall. But because, unlike every other time he'd brought one of his problems – private, professional, or most often, a problem caused by mixing the two – this time, Marshall hadn't suggested any solutions.

'It's all here,' Hugh said, retrieving another sheet of paper. 'Stock ownership by demographic. Ninety-four percent of families with a net worth in the top 10% own stocks, compared to 21% in the bottom quarter. White families are three times as likely to own stocks. Ownership rates are highest among the middle aged, and those over 65 own close to half of the entire value of the stock market,' he quoted. 'So all you need to do,' Hugh concluded, 'is ensure the right people wind up on the jury.'

Marshall held his gaze for a moment. 'Wealthy, white, and wizened?'

Hugh thought he detected a spark in Marshall's eye. As if he were beginning to see a way forward at last.

'Exactly! A jury of our peers!'

'Hugh,' Marshall paused for a moment. 'You are peerless.'

Now that was a quote Hugh could see on the cover of his book: 'peerless'. He liked the sound of that.

'Your income places you in the 99th percentile,' Marshall continued. 'Even with the most careful jury selection, with the most highly-paid jury consultants, the odds of getting a jury with those demographics are astronomically against us.'

'Sure, that's true of direct shareholders. But what about all those who invest indirectly? Their views are represented at shareholders' meetings too. Fund managers are always voting in favor of our compensation packages. Surely that translates to a general endorsement from the public?'

Marshall slid the article back. 'Did you read this? It says right here, pension funds and financial managers have failed investors for decades, by acting as, and I quote, "rubber stamps" rather than holding corporations accountable for the excessive compensation they've awarded CEOs.'

The way Marshall said it, he made rubber-stamping sound like a bad thing, instead of the board's bread-and-butter.

'Mr. Marshall? Your three o'clock is here.'

'Hugh,' Marshall picked up his portfolio, 'I'm afraid I won't be able to represent you.'

'What?' Hugh spluttered.

'As you know, all company employees – yourselves included – are employed 'at will'. It is entirely legal for the company to fire you at any time, and without cause.'

Marshall was right. After all, he'd helped Hugh and the rest of the board lobby against proposed changes to that very law just a year ago.

'Maybe we can appeal to the shareholders then?'

Marshall shook his head. 'You made shareholder votes non-binding. Since the algorithm is programmed to keep running things like it did in the past, the most likely scenario is that the AutoCEO will continue to ignore shareholder opinion. You can't sue Mike J. Guy. And as far as AutoAutomator is concerned… I just can't see that I'd be able to mount a decent case for you there, either.'

Hugh could feel the hair on the back of his neck sticking up.

This wasn't about the merits of the case. He was sure of it.

Marshall just wanted to distance himself from Hugh and the rest of the board, now that they weren't on top.

'What is this Marshall? You working for CGM?' It occurred, belatedly, to Hugh that he should have asked this question at the beginning of their meeting.

Marshall shook his head.

'Can you refer me to someone else in the firm then?' Marshall, Marshall and Williamson was an enormous law firm. Surely there was someone more competent than Marshall who was willing to take on their case Hugh thought, his suspicions that Marshall was beginning to lose the plot confirmed. He supposed that was what happened when you inherited not only your first car and your first company, but your first lawyer from your father: they all broke down, went broke, or had a breakdown prematurely.

'I've already asked around,' Marshall looked down. He paused. 'I really can't see this working on your own. I think your best chance would be to file a class action lawsuit. Have you tried the union?'

Hugh could feel his blood pressure rising. His doctor had warned him he was in bad shape, but he never thought he'd feel the blood struggle to force its way through his hardened heart quite so strongly. 'You have to represent me!' Hugh spluttered. 'We have a contract!'

Marshall turned, silhouetted in the doorway. 'My contract is with the company.'

'I am the company!'

CHAPTER 9

Hugh kicked FouFou off the bed. She was his ex's dog, really, but just like the sheets, Hugh had gotten to keep FouFou in the settlement.

Hugh wasn't sure which he hated most – the dog, or the haberdashery. Bambi had insisted upon white curtains and sheets with frills, and a million and one different throw cushions on top of the bed. Hugh had kept every single one of them. Even the heart-shaped cushion with the lace trim she'd caught him getting down and dirty with Kira on.

Of course, Bambi had put up all sorts of arguments as to why Hugh shouldn't get the dog – even though he had no idea why anyone would want the damn yappy thing. He was never around to take her for walks. He wouldn't give FouFou her medicine at the proper times. The list - just like Bambi herself - went on and on. But somehow, Marshall had counterarguments for every one of them.

Marshall. Hugh could feel his heart burn. How could he have betrayed him like this? Hugh felt sure it was because of the company. He didn't buy for an instant that a lawyer like Marshall, one who could fight tooth and nail to win a case as hopeless as his fight for FouFou, wouldn't be able to win a case as obviously in his favor as this one.

Hugh walked into the bathroom, wrapping himself in Bambi's robe. He did this not to feel close to her – the robe had been laundered many times since she'd last worn it – but because the warm feeling of having won surpassed the warmth his own matching robe could provide.

Brushing his teeth, Hugh glanced across to the second sink, where Bambi's expensive face creams and perfumes remained exactly where they had been when she last used them. Even her toothbrush was still in its holder. By the time Marshall was done with her, Bambi realized it was easier to just leave it all behind.

He froze, mouth full of foam, and hit the OFF button on his toothbrush. He didn't need any more damn robots getting ideas above their station. Was this where it had all begun? Had the machines gotten sick of removing the built-up plaque, caviar residue, and pickle shards from between Hugh's molars and risen up to eliminate them all – or worse – unionize?

Spitting into Bambi's sink – he never used his own, much as he never used his own toilet – Hugh resolved to find a lawyer who would destroy AutoAutomator.

Hugh wandered downstairs for coffee. A coffee he'd make himself, thank you very much. At least, that was his plan – until he realized all of his King Jantan peaberry coffee came in little pods which he didn't know how to open without inserting them into the machine. Then he remembered – the Black Ivory beans he had specially flown in each month.

'Lucia!' he roared, robe flapping open as his floor heating started automatically. 'Make me a coffee!' Really, Bambi's robe was both too small and too short for him, but Hugh never minded a bit of breeze.

He settled into his comfortable massage chair by the window. His coffee would be made the old-fashioned way.

By a poorly paid immigrant. Not some uppity new-fangled machine.

That, Hugh realized, was the problem with machines.

They didn't have feelings.

Feelings that you could manipulate, to keep them in their place.

Speaking of feelings, Hugh stared at his phone, Marshall's words echoing through his head.

The union.

A class action lawsuit.

The last thing Hugh felt like doing was talking to Lila, or any 'lawyers' she might recommend – if indeed she would recommend anyone to Hugh.

But the second-to-last thing Hugh felt like doing was talking to the board. Not after they'd all worked out that the real reason he'd recommended the AutoAutomator that had cost them their jobs was because he was getting laid and paid by Kira.

The betrayal Hugh felt when Marshall turned down his case was almost as bad as the betrayal he'd felt when he found out Pete had sold off all his shares in CGM.

Pete. That's who he'd call first. After all, Pete owed him. Or at a minimum, their sins against each other canceled out. And once he'd gotten Pete on board, he'd win the others back.

'Myra,' Hugh commanded. 'Call Pete.'

For once, Pete answered right away. And he was only too eager to hear how Hugh's meeting with Marshall had turned out.

'Sure, the jury will be mostly made up of workers,' he agreed. 'But they're also stockholders for the most part. Around 50% of people directly hold shares, and that's before you consider everyone who owns stocks through a mutual fund or retirement plan. And I think we know a thing or two about getting shareholders to vote with us. Our compensation packages are approved by shareholders!'

It was Hugh's turn to shift uncomfortably. His last package hadn't been approved by a majority of shareholders – but the board had overridden their decision anyway. That was the whole point of having your friends on the board, he bristled. They were loyal. They repaid favors. At least, they were meant to.

Now wasn't the time to bring that up, Hugh reminded himself. Now that things had failed so spectacularly with Marshall, he needed to keep Pete on his side, to get the others on board too.

CHAPTER 10

'The first part is problematic,' Joe Joseph, attorney at law said. He paused to wipe the ketchup from his hands onto his trouser legs. 'But this second clause? That's golden. "Beneficial". That one word,' he declared, smacking the last of the ketchup from his index finger and holding it in the air, 'is the part that will save your bacon.'

This was, Hugh mused, exactly what he knew an ambulance-chaser like Joe Joseph, with an office next to a laundromat and a waiting area replete with trashy magazines and discarded neck braces, would say about that word when Lila had insisted upon its insertion. Of course he would. After all, Joseph was the union lawyer Lila had put him onto.

This exact scenario – a group of disgruntled former employees huddled in the cramped offices of a lawyer who advertised his services on park benches and the sides of buses – was exactly the situation Hugh had been afraid of when he'd signed the final contract.

The only difference was that Hugh had imagined himself at the pointy end of a class-action lawsuit. Not the one hiring someone like Joe Joseph after every other lawyer in town – and several interstate – had turned him down.

'Fortunately,' Joseph continued, 'the contract specifies that immediate financial gains alone are insufficient to outsource or, in your case, automate, a position. The software must demonstrate that the company will also derive substantial benefits on other measures. Lowered risk, or public relations gains – more qualitative aspects which may not immediately translate to dollars and cents, but will contribute to long-term value.'

'It's an open-and-shut case,' Kim leaned back in his chair. Kim should know, Hugh thought. He'd had his own fair share of lawsuits. Almost all of PearShape's early code had been 'borrowed' in one way or another, and yet, it remained one of the most profitable companies on earth. Not only had they managed to retain the rights to technology they hadn't developed, but PearShape's lawyers had managed to convince the courts that placing electronics in a rectangular box was their intellectual property. And that a fresh fruit retailer should be prevented from using a pear on its logo. 'All we have to do is demonstrate our value.'

'But how do we do that?' Parker frowned, squirming in his seat. At least he had a seat. Hugh and Deborah were standing in Joseph's cramped office.

'Our letters!' Kim cried. 'Not only do they outline our achievements, but – just a second, I've got an article about it somewhere...' He rifled through a stack of papers in his briefcase. Every morning, Hugh knew, Kim got his assistant to print out the day's finance headlines from PearShapeNews+.

'Here it is! "CEO letters have been shown to affect share price".'

Joseph took the page. 'CEO letters have been shown to affect share price,' he read aloud, 'when well-written letters are compared to poorly written ones. The majority of letters, however, have no effect.' He looked up from the page, adjusting his glasses. 'In other words, the company might as well not release any letter at all.'

'Surely it would look suspicious if they stopped releasing letters!' Parker protested.

'I'm certain the AutoAutomator will have factored that into its calculations,' Joseph waved a hand. 'It will have analyzed the common features of the best CEO letters, then pulled together the most applicable bits to create tailored letters.'

Hugh had to admit, the Auto-Automator-authored letter was better than anything he'd ever written.

Or rather, anything he'd ever been in charge of writing.

'Who knew machines could write letters?' Kim cried, head in hands.

'Remember that animated paperclip that used to pop up whenever you'd type "Dear such-and-such" or "To whom it may concern?" Parker grumbled. Hugh certainly remembered – he'd been looking for that little bastard when he first attempted to type out his memoirs. 'I'll bet that's what started it all!'

'Machines have been writing reports for years,' Joseph said. 'Human-written letters are a liability. True, a well-written letter might make the share price go up. But the risk of a poorly-written letter causing a decrease in stock price is just too high.'

Joseph didn't need to finish his statement. It hung in the air without ever leaving his mouth. The company was demonstrably better off without a CEO in this context.

'Come on,' Parker urged again. 'We should be good at this! Collectively, we employ over six million people. We should be experts at evaluating performance! How do we demonstrate our own?'

'Benchmarking!' Hugh spluttered, wiping his brow. The dust-clogged air-conditioner balanced on Joseph's windowsill was making a lot of noise, but failing to cope with the collective heat of the board.

'Good, good. But who do we benchmark ourselves against?'

'Each other.'

'I don't think that's going to work this time,' Deborah interjected. 'Since we've all been replaced. What about the CEOs of other companies? Ones that still have their jobs?'

The ones who were smart enough not to use AutoAutomator, she was implying. Hugh knew Deborah would be the stick in the mud. The others were much more understanding about how easily Kira had convinced Hugh to trial the software.

'I don't think what any of us do is comparable to what any other CEO does,' Hugh jumped in. 'Our industries are so variable… How is what I do similar to what David McKing does in the fast food industry, or what Howard Mall does in retail?'

'Hugh's right,' Parker nodded so vigorously, Hugh was afraid his toupee might fly off. Only Hugh knew that his hair wasn't really his. Then again, Pete's teeth weren't his own, and neither were Kim's silicon-sculpted calves, so Hugh didn't know what he was worried about. 'The market forces affecting our performances are totally different.'

Joseph frowned. 'The crux of this case is that you guys are worth every penny you're paid. We're going to have to demonstrate the value you add to the company. The benefit you bring, irrespective of market forces. That the key variable – or at least a key variable – in the company's success is your decision making. Most importantly, we need to demonstrate that you provide value that your computerized counterparts can never hope to emulate.'

He tapped his pen against his yellow legal pad. The page, Hugh was alarmed to see, was empty other than a ketchup smear and what looked disturbingly like a half-finished game of hangman. Hugh hoped against all reason that Joseph was one of those savant guys who looked like a mess, but had a brilliant mind whirring away underneath.

'What about shareholder's meetings?' Joseph continued. 'They're a chance for investors to put a face to a name. To see that you're real human beings.' He paused to write this phrase down, and underline it. 'I'll need some statistics on attendance,' he mused, 'to show engagement has been rising.'

'I'm not sure that will be possible,' Hugh hedged. He sensed this was no time to admit that he and the rest of the board were competing for the lowest annual meeting attendance.

'No sweat. Rising attendance isn't a big deal. Most things are going virtual these days. We don't need numbers. It's the principle of the matter.'

Confidence surged in Hugh's chest for the first time in a long time. Now this guy was speaking his language.

'So what do you need from us?'

'Evidence. Qualitative evidence. We argue that, by focusing exclusively on the numbers, on quantitative data, the AutoAutomator has miscalculated the AutoCEO's benefits to the company, and underestimated your collective contributions.'

'So we go up there and spin a lot of BS? Get some of our PR people on to it?'

'We no longer have PR people,' Deborah corrected. 'Our *former* companies have PR people.'

'Qualitative data doesn't mean airy fairy,' Joseph frowned. 'We need concrete evidence of the value you bring to your companies. Employee or customer testimonials. Survey data. Interviews'.

He sprang up from his squeaky chair, but his office was so narrow, his pacing amounted to shuffling the length of just two peeling carpet tiles.

'Analyses of your managerial methodologies. Academic studies of the philosophies underpinning your decision-making processes!'

Joseph returned to his seat, the rusty office chair squealing under his weight. He was a heavyset man, but with more of the multi-ringed physique that resulted from poor nutrition than the barrel-like rotundness of Hugh's well-fed portly class.

'I'm not talking about a marketing spiel,' Joseph slammed his hands on the desk, leaving vaguely ketchup-colored prints on the contract. 'But a nuanced argument. One that shows human CEOs are capable of the compassion, flexibility, and innovation that computers will never be!'

Hugh tasted blood, then realized he'd bitten his tongue.

He'd spent years – his whole career – striving to eliminate compassion. To be consistent. Conservative. Perhaps a computer was as good at empathy as he was.

His ex-wife and daughter certainly thought so.

'Essentially,' Joseph smiled, revealing a gold tooth, 'you are the figureheads of your companies. Celebrities!'

'What do you mean?'

'Like the royal family. Everybody loves them!'

Hugh thought back to the trashy magazines in Joseph's waiting room. It was true – even here, in the land of the free.

And wasn't he a form of home-grown royalty?

PART 2

CHAPTER 11

Seated in the courthouse, dressed in the cheap suit Joseph had insisted he buy, Hugh felt on familiar turf – and not just because he had gotten used to the inside of courthouses over the past year or so. Sure, he didn't have an entire team of lawyers at his disposal this time. He had something better – the members of his board. And for the first time, he was sure of their loyalty, for their fates were bound as tightly to the outcome of this case as were his.

The depositions had gone well. Better than expected, really. Hugh and his fellow CEOs had squeezed into a room above a gymnasium Joe Joseph had rented by the hour. Certainly, Hugh and the rest of the board could have afforded somewhere more cushy to give their statements and answer questions. But the anonymity of the Central Squash Courts Community Room B suited them nicely. Hugh felt he'd handled the questions quite well, especially considering he wasn't able to use his favored strategy of pawning them off to subordinates.

His confidence in Joseph had grown, too, when he arranged for Hugh to be able to use his own backdrop for the recordings – a copy of the mottled brown tones the photographer usually brought in for his head shots. As he settled into the uncomfortable plastic chair, straining to hear Joseph's instructions over the squeak of rubber soles on cheap parquetry, and balls smashing into walls, Hugh couldn't help but think of Maddy.

She should have been there, primping and fussing over him, getting the right angle, adjusting his hair, making sure his portrait looked perfect. The one which would appear on his book jacket, that was. Hugh was after something much more dynamic for the front cover. Something modeled off one of Skum's dramatic poses on one of his many biographies. Skydiving, or jet skiing.

Of course, Hugh had never accomplished any of these feats. But it was marvelous what you could do with a computer these days. He knew that, because of the vast sums of money he'd paid some expert to stitch his son's head onto some water polo player's body years ago, after he'd failed every exam across the board. The only way for Hugh J. Richardson Jnr. IV to get into college, even with his father's connections, was by pretending to have some extra-curricular talent.

Hugh swallowed, wishing he was sitting in front of his familiar mottled background now. His eyes started to water as he saw Maddy, not gazing at him admiringly, leaning over to adjust his tie, but sitting there, pen poised, ready to jot down all of the unflattering things he was sure the opposing counsel was about to say about him.

Instead, it was Joseph who leaned in, so close Hugh could smell the egg-and-onion burrito he'd had for breakfast.

'I imagine we'll get through this all very quickly.' Joseph smiled. There was, Hugh noticed, a little egg on his tie, and a little onion in his teeth. Even so, the breadth of his grin was reassuring, even if the scent and color of it was not. 'They've come up with hardly any witnesses, and none of them pose a threat.'

Hugh felt his muscles loosen. 'Who are we up against?' he whispered back. To be honest, he hadn't been paying much attention before – hadn't want to pay much attention.

'A programmer from AutoAutomator. You should have seen him in the deposition! Nervous as hell! I'm surprised they're even letting him take the stand.'

'Who else?' Hugh asked, cursing the urgency he could feel seeping into his voice.

'Some union leader!' Joseph's voice rose above a whisper. 'Can you believe it?'

Hugh couldn't. Was there anyone less trustworthy than a union leader? Surely the court would see through that.

'And last,' Joseph's smile grew even wider, wide enough that Hugh could see a piece of parsley stuck to one of his fillings. 'Their "star expert" is some musty professor! Not even Ivy League. Not even from a business school! A social sciences department!'

Something churned in Hugh's belly. It must be the stench of Joseph's breath affecting him.

Joseph adjusted his eggy tie and stood up to deliver his opening statements.

CHAPTER 12

'Please state your name and occupation for the record.'

'Hugh J. Richardson. CEO-' Hugh's voice caught in his throat as he looked across at Pete, and then, towards Maddy. 'Former CEO of CGM.'

'The court will enter Mr. Richardson's current occupation as unemployed.'

Hugh wanted to object, but he was pretty sure that was the lawyer's job, and also, that it wouldn't go down too well with the judge. The collar on his terrible suit was already beginning to scratch his neck. Still, he knew Joseph's advice was sound. He needed to look 'relatable'.

It was just the sort of thing Maddy would have said.

Joseph ran through the rest of the questions, and Hugh answered them, just like they'd rehearsed. This, Hugh thought, was how press interviews and shareholder meetings ought to be held. With a selected individual asking a predetermined list of questions in a sympathetic manner. He hoped Maddy was getting all this down, certain he was making a good impression.

Everything was going well in fact. Or at least, as well as Hugh could hope, given he was embroiled in his second court case in less than twelve months. Third, if you counted that whole harassment thing, which hadn't quite progressed to the courtroom, thanks to a briefcase full of cash.

At least, Hugh imagined there had been a briefcase full of cash. Several, in fact. Though he supposed it was, more likely, all done via bank transfer.

Even settling the sexual harassment cases your employees brought against you had been ruined by computers. All the fun of darting around with bags of cash had been sucked out of the slightly gray areas of corporate life, in favor of shifting a few numbers on a spreadsheet.

Hugh was just about to rise from his seat when Marshall stood. His blood chilled. Enchanted by his own charisma, Hugh had forgotten that the court would give the defense a turn, too.

He stared at Marshall, hoping that his eyes conveyed the full extent of his sense of betrayal. When he was CEO again, Hugh's first action would be to fire Marshall, Marshall and Williamson. Publicly. Press releases and social media statements danced in front of his eyes. Maybe he'd even make an announcement from a podium.

'Mr. Richardson, in the statement you gave at your deposition, you described yourself as "the face of the company," correct?'

Hugh nodded. Joseph had come up with that line. At first, he'd tried describing himself as 'the king of the company', given what Joseph had said about CEOs being like royalty. But Joseph had told him that probably wouldn't play well in court. He also vetoed 'emperor' and 'lord'. So, 'face of the company' it was.

'Mr. Richardson, please identify this object for the court.'

Hugh gulped. His mind raced. His eyes lost focus.

What could be on it?

Surely not his private games as Pedro the Pool Boy, or Ahmed the Airconditioner Repairman. He racked his brain, trying to think of what happened to that tape. Could Bambi have taken it? He was sure he'd had his security stop her from taking anything from the house.

'Mr. Richardson?'

'It would appear to be a video cassette.'

'Could you please read the label?'

Hugh squinted, relief coursing through his veins.

'*Secret CEO*: Audition #484.'

Hugh's relief was short-lived.

'And the rest?'

'H. J. Richardson'

The squeal as the ancient television and video player was wheeled into the courtroom was almost as excruciating as watching the footage it displayed when Marshall pushed the cassette into the decrepit machine.

'Mr. Richardson, is it fair to describe yourself as the 'face of the company' when even employees at your own company fail to recognize you?'

'Objection! The entire premise of *Secret CEO* is that employees don't recognize their employer. It's hardly uncommon. In any case, this video is more than a decade old – it's on literal tape! My client has spent years developing in his role, at an entirely different firm, since this film was shot.'

'Perhaps you'd prefer this more recent data. Mr. Richardson, when employees at your current company were shown this lineup earlier this year, isn't it true that almost half were unable to indicate which was their company's leader?'

Hugh stared at the images. 'They're all middle-aged white men, like me!' he spluttered. 'Of course they couldn't figure out which one was me, we all look alike! This lineup is rigged!'

Hugh had heard of stereotyping and racial profiling before - several of his employees had even accused the company of it. But he'd never thought he would be the victim of such blatant discrimination.

'Mr. Richardson, this is your board photograph. You chose the lineup.'

Hugh squinted. Now that he looked closely, he could make out some of the familiar faces.

Truth be told, even he didn't recognize everyone on the page. Most of the members, like the inner circle who'd joined him in this case, were there to stack the deck in his favor. But there were plenty of others who he'd recruited simply because their names looked good in print.

'Mr. Richardson, you were a member of Mr. Harding's board, and vice-versa. Is that correct?'

'Yes, that's right.'

'At the last general meeting of Mr. Harding's company, do you recall a group of shareholders coming forward with a proposal for corporate sponsorship for a foundation supporting the highly endangered shrinkbody spinemouse?'

'Yes.' Hugh remembered them all right. A bunch of long-haired and bearded idiots who probably only owned about four shares between them. He wondered whether that was the same animal the protesters outside CGM's meeting had been going on about.

'Do you recall how the board justified the rejection of this proposal, without first taking it to a shareholder vote?'

'Not at this time.'

'Let me refresh your memory,' Marshall picked up a copy of the minutes. 'Allow me to quote: 'There are frequent calls for companies to undertake more charity, and while the board is sympathetic to this view, we believe corporations are not the appropriate conduit for charitable works, for the simple reason that corporate money does not belong to the CEO, or to the board, but to the shareholders. As the board of Hardings, we are entrusted with the stewardship of your money as shareholders, and it is our primary duty to return as much of the money you have entrusted to us as possible. Individual shareholders may then make their own charitable contributions using these returns. In sum, it would be inappropriate for the board to make these decisions on behalf of individual shareholders.'''

Hugh leaned back in his chair. That was quite well-phrased, he thought. Having his own words – or at least, words attributed to him – read back to him was surprisingly pleasing.

'Sounds about right,' he said.

'Well then. Can you explain why you do not apply this same logic to compensation? Why is it that your primary objective, when it comes to setting compensation packages, appears to be maximizing CEO pay at the expense of shareholder's returns? Even in direct opposition to shareholders' stated wishes?'

'I wouldn't call that my primary objective.' It certainly was, but Hugh wouldn't call it that.

'Mr. Richardson, in your previous occupation, what were you paid?'

Hugh stared at him. Marshall knew full well what he earned. Why was he asking him this? To belittle how much he earned, in comparison to the other board members?

Then Hugh remembered what Joseph had said in their coaching: "To most people, thirty-eight million is a lot of money.'

'Mr. Richardson?'

'Thirty-eight million,' he mumbled.

'Could you repeat that?'

'Thirty-eight million.' Hugh looked around, to see if any of his fellow CEOs were scoffing at his paltry sum. Straining to see if Maddy was writing down anything unflattering.

'Thirty-eight million!' Marshall repeated, as if in shock. Usually, Hugh relished watching the jury eat out of Marshall's hand. Today, he was completely unamused by his theatrics. 'And was that the totality of your annual compensation?'

'Thank you for your question.' Hugh smiled the winning smile he practiced in the mirror each morning. The one he used to dazzle investors and reporters. 'I appreciate you asking, but I'm not going to answer that. I'll take the next question.'

'Mr. Richardson, may I remind you, you are under oath!'

Even Joseph was glowering at him. This wasn't what they'd rehearsed.

'I'll repeat the question,' Marshall said. 'Is that the totality of your annual compensation?'

'No,' Hugh swallowed. 'I received bonuses and so on, up to the value of about fifty million.'

How Hugh wished he'd gotten his raise. Then he would have been able to say his base pay was fifty-two million. With the bonuses, he'd be pushing sixty – a far more respectable sum.

Then again, given what Joseph had told him about the 'average guy', perhaps it was a good thing he hadn't. Joe Joseph was a diamond in the rough in that regard, Hugh concluded. He could do something Marshall never could – help him relate to the average 'guy on the street'.

'Did you receive any other perks?'

Hugh looked at Joseph. He was glowering again.

'Yes. I had the use of the company jet. A vehicle and driver.'

'And the company's island holiday home, and ski chalet, and golf course?'

Hugh narrowed his eyes. The only reason Marshall knew about the company villas was because Hugh himself had invited Marshall there to stay.

'Yes.'

'Mr. Richardson, how many days did you spend at those properties over the last year?'

'I'm afraid I don't recall.'

'A rough estimate will do. Approximately how much of your time did you spend in the office, and how much on vacation?'

'I'm afraid I don't recall.'

'Perhaps this will refresh your memory.'

Hugh stared at the page in front of him.

'How did you get this? This is private!'

'Your Myra digital assistant data? It was part of discovery. And part of the data collected by the AutoAutomator software.'

Hugh scowled.

'Let me ask you again, Mr. Richardson. How many days did you spend at those properties over the last year?'

'One hundred and eleven.'

'That's just the number of days you spent on the golf course, isn't it?'

'Yes.'

'What about the villa? The chalet?'

They went through all of the properties. Hugh felt each blow viscerally. Not just because it was bad for the case. But because it was a sharp reminder of what he'd lost. What he would lose forever, if Joseph didn't find some way to turn this case around.

CHAPTER 13

Hugh stewed while the other board members – the closest thing he had to friends – took their turns at the stand.

Arms folded across his chest, feet firmly planted on the floor, his mouth turned down, Hugh hardly heard a word of their answers. Joseph had to practically drag him out of the courtroom after the judge declared a break for lunch.

Lunch. Hugh could barely think about eating as he stuffed his mouth with foie gras, forcing it down his gullet just for the sake of appearances. He was grateful for the restaurant's mood lighting, hiding the emotions he was sure were playing across his face.

L'oie Pompeuse had always been Hugh's favorite establishment for dates, the ambience flattering to almost anyone – something that both worked to Hugh's advantage in disguising his own features, and making those of others more palatable to himself.

Only Kim seemed to be thinking about anything other than the case, thumbing through *The Yew Herald*. Why he couldn't just read the news on his phone like a normal person, Hugh didn't know. Probably, he was beginning to suspect, because Kim didn't know how to get the news on his phone.

In any case, Kim was desperate to see whether his son's third wedding had warranted a mention (it hadn't), and whether his rival, Dan Wang's recent adoption of a dog called Britches had (it had).

'How come people like Wang haven't lost their jobs?' Kim grumbled, spreading the *Herald* out, society pages on one side, the book list on the other.

Hugh's eyes widened, and not just because of all the foie gras he was force-feeding himself.

There, at the top of the list, he saw a familiar title.

Immediately, he called Maddy.

'You dark horse! You didn't tell me you'd finished the book!'

'Finished the book?'

'And you didn't do a bad job!' Hugh exclaimed, something stinging his eyes. Number one!

It wouldn't be accurate to say Hugh hadn't dreamed it – heck, even expected it. He had. Of course he had. Before he'd written a word, before he'd met Maddy to write his words for him, Hugh had commissioned one company that would guarantee his book pride of place in bookstores and online shops, and another that would send in swathes of shoppers to buy his book up in such volume, it was assured to rocket to the very top of the charts.

But this was something else.

For the first time, Hugh felt a real sense of pride.

He had gotten to number one based solely upon his own merits for the very first time.

It was there, his name in print. Or rather, the name of his book in print: '*A Way to Build a Company, a Way to Build a Life, and a Way to Build a Unified Way*'. It really did have everything. Hugh doubted one of AutoAutomator's fancy algorithms could have picked a better title. Sure, the title was so long, the subtitle (A Memoir of Hugh J. Richardson, CEO of CGM) was truncated. But he had made it, at last.

After all the bad news of recent months, finally, something was going his way.

'Hugh? What are you talking about?'

'*A Way to Build a Company*. It's number one on the *Yew Herald* Bestseller list!'

There was silence as Maddy, presumably, looked up the list online. Hugh looked around the table, expecting to find the others basking in his spotlight, but only Pete showed a skerrick of interest. Deborah was on her phone, Kim was bitterly mumbling threats aimed at Wang's dog, and Parker's attention was directed at the bouillabaisse he'd slopped on his shirtfront.

'Do you see it?' Hugh's left foot tapped impatiently.

'I see *A Way to Build a Company*. But it's not your book. Did you check the author's name?'

Hugh pulled Dan's paper back towards him, straining to make out the letters in the candlelight.

There it was, in the fine print underneath the title: Mike J. Guy.

Was there anything the man – or machine – had not stolen from him?

'How can he do this?' Hugh roared, spilling his drink across the table. Now he had everyone's attention. Kim leapt up, shaking the sodden pictures of Britches. Hugh would have thought he'd be only too pleased to see them ruined. 'That's copyright infringement, surely!'

he continued.

Hugh's heart leapt. Copyright infringement was another log he could throw on the fire, another charge he could add to the ticket, to take this Mike J. Guy down. This could only go in his favor.

'No,' Maddy said softly.

A terrible thought struck Hugh: Had Maddy written the book? Had she switched sides? Why else would Mike's book use the same title? And how else could it have been written so quickly?

'What do you mean? It's the exact same title. The title you – I mean we – came up with!'

'Not really,' Maddy explained. 'The title was generated by artificial intelligence.'

Hugh had been called stupid before, by his ex-wife, his children. Even by his own parents. But to describe his intelligence as artificial? That was a new low.

'What do you mean?' he demanded.

'It's how we come up with all of our non-fiction titles these days. You feed a few keywords into the program, and bingo, out pops the most marketable combination.'

'But- but-' Hugh spluttered, 'How can Mike J. Guy have an autobiography? Auto means self!' Hugh was pleased that, for once, his classics training had proved useful. 'He doesn't even have a self to write about!'

Maddy exhaled. 'My guess,' she said, 'is that the publisher used AI to write the whole thing.'

CHAPTER 14

'My name is Jana Dryser, and I am a compensation consultant at ExtremeUnlimited.'

'What is a compensation consultant?'

'Essentially, I partner with boards, bringing data and experience to the table to help compensation committees, boards, and shareholders make informed decisions regarding, in this instance, the compensation of a CEO. It's a cyclical role, involving ongoing consultation, research, and reporting.'

'Ms. Dryser, can you identify the document dated August third, please?'

'Certainly,' Jana smiled. 'This is the report I submitted in support of Mr. Richardson's compensation review.'

'And Ms. Dryser, can you please read the final line?' Joseph asked, fiddling with his tie. Red, with blue stripes. The very sort of tie Hugh used to wear when representing CGM – though, he now noticed, with a sauce stain as well as the egg splatter where a tie clip should have been.

Hugh stared as Jana turned to the last page of the report. The report she was supposed to have read out at the shareholder meeting, had Mike J. Guy not taken over.

The woman who was supposed to have argued for Hugh's raise was now arguing for him to keep any income at all. He wondered if he'd have to pay her extra for her expert witness testimony, or whether Joe Joseph had managed to negotiate her appearance as part of her existing fee.

'In conclusion,' Jana quoted, 'I recommend that the shareholders adjust Mr. Richardson's base salary by thirty-six point eight percent.'

'Was that adjustment down or up?'

Jana smiled her winning smile. 'Up, of course. One theory of CEO pay suggests that compensation corresponds to the degree of confidence the board has in their choice of CEO. A confident board and a confident CEO should produce confidence in shareholders, which will, in turn, drive up the stock price – and that's good news for everyone.'

'So Ms. Dryser, you, in your extensive professional experience, determined that not only was Mr. Richardson worth his pay, but that he was deserving of thirty-eight point six percent more than he was being paid at the time he was made redundant?'

'Precisely.'

At least Jana was doing well, even if Joseph looked a mess.

At least, that was, until Marshall rose from his chair again.

'Ms. Dryser, you get paid to tell people how much to pay other people, correct?'

Jana's pearly whites disappeared into a tight-lipped smile. 'It's more sophisticated than that, but broadly speaking, yes.'

Marshall shuffled some papers, then held up a copy of the report.

'You recommended that Mr. Richardson's pay be increased?'

'Yes, by thirty-eight point six percent.'

'And what does that translate to, in dollars and cents? I'm not the best at math,' Marshall smiled. Hugh scowled. He knew full well that Marshall had an outstanding education in mathematics. How dare he try and appeal to the lowest common denominator like this? Appealing to the poor – and the poorly educated – was supposed to be Joseph's secret power!

'It would be in the ballpark of fourteen,' Jana stared at her manicured nails.

'Fourteen thousand dollars?' Marshall feigned shock. 'That's as much as some of Mr. Richardson's employees make per year!'

A slight cough. 'Fourteen million.'

'You recommended that Mr. Richardson, whose base salary was thirty-eight million dollars, be paid an additional fourteen million per year? Bringing his total pay to fifty-two million?'

'Yes.'

'How did you justify this recommendation? What methods did you use to observe and measure Mr. Richardson's performance?'

'My methods are more indirect-'

'So that's a no? You did not observe Mr. Richardson's performance in his role? Evaluate his work?'

'I analyzed the compensation packages of CEOs with similar levels of experience, in comparably sized firms, and in similar fields.'

'Were any of these CEOs used for comparison also members of the

CGM board?'

'Yes, a number of them were. It is not unusual for CEOs to serve on the boards of other companies – they have a great deal of expertise to share.'

'And did you also act as a compensation consultant in relation to any of these other CEOs' pay at their respective companies?'

'Yes. Compensation consulting at the C-suite level is a highly specialized field, and I have provided services for many of the nation's top companies.'

'Can you name those companies for the court?'

'Well, Hardings. And PearShape. And ToyStar. And PharmaX, among others.'

'And what happens when you have made your – what did you call it – comparisons?'

'Usually, I provide the compensation committee with a recommended range, rather than a single answer.'

'And how do you define compensation?'

'A CEO's compensation package might comprise their base salary, bonuses, stocks or stock options, and any job-related perks.'

'What sort of perks?'

'Financial planning services might be one example, or the use of a company car.'

'Or a corporate jet? What about a holiday home, or country club membership?'

'Well, yes, I suppose-'

'And these are considered job-related?'

'Of course,' Jana smoothed her skirt, a manicured fingernail catching the fabric. 'A car is necessary for work-related travel, and naturally, an individual with a substantial income will be in need of financial planning.'

'Wouldn't the-' Marshall checked his notes - 'five thousand eight hundred and ninety two PearShape and ToyStar employees earning less than the federal minimum wage be in greater need of assistance with financial planning than a CEO earning two thousand times what they do?'

Jana gripped her glass of water so fiercely, Hugh was afraid it might shatter. 'On the contrary, a larger income means a dramatically increased burden in terms of financial management.'

'What about the burden of an unexpected health emergency? Do the companies you work with ensure that all staff have access to financial planning services?'

'Not that I am aware of. Though there are plenty of faith-based charities and for-profit groups which offer financial assistance either free or for a fee.'

'In other words, CEOs with tens or hundreds millions of dollars can receive high-quality financial advice, paid for by the company, while their employees who have limited funds and are most in need of advice on maximizing their income and savings, have to find the time to actively seek out advice, either from charitable volunteer organizations already stretched thin, with an agenda to push, or from predatory groups that take advantage of those with limited options.'

'Objection!' Joseph finally sprang to action. 'Ms. Dryser is not on trial for the financial woes of the poor!'

'You introduced her to the stand in her capacity as a compensation consultant – an expert in what people should be paid!'

'Ms. Dryser is a compensation consultant to C-level executives,'

Joseph shot back.

'Sustained. Please restrict your questions to the domain of Ms. Dryser's specialization.'

'Fine,' Marshall acquiesced. 'Ms. Dryser, can you explain how these perks might be "work-related"?'

Jana fidgeted with the ring on her finger. 'Mr. Richardson's jet might be used to travel between meetings. And the holiday home and country club to entertain clients. Most major deals at this level occur through personal connections rather than a tendering process.'

'Just like the hiring of CEOs and their boards, correct?'

'Well, yes.' The diamond in Jana's ring caught the fluorescent courtroom lights.

'Ms. Dryser, you testified that your recommendation usually takes the form of a range. Can you please describe a typical range?'

'After collecting data from CEOs with similar levels of expertise and experience at similar companies, I might determine a range of one to one hundred million, with an average of approximately twenty-four million in base compensation.'

'One to one hundred million? That's a rather large range, isn't it?'

'Well, compensation consulting is qualitative,' Jana smiled. Hugh was relieved to see she'd apparently regained enough composure to turn on the charm he'd been relying on to win over the shareholders. 'You might say it's more art than science.' That! That was exactly the argument Hugh had been waiting for. That his value couldn't be evaluated by some machine!

'But ultimately, Ms. Dryser, you are paid to put a figure on a CEO's value to the company, correct?'

'Yes.'

'What differentiates a CEO worth, say, one million a year, from the CEO earning one hundred million? Do they put in just one percent of the effort? Work just one percent of the hours? Achieve just one percent of the results?'

'CEOs in general tend to be extremely dedicated and driven individuals-'

'Yes or no, Ms. Dryser. Does a CEO paid one hundred million a year put in one hundred times the work of a CEO paid just one million?'

'No. The relationship is not necessarily linear.'

'How about the specific case of Mr. Richardson?'

'I presented the compensation committee with a range commensurate with Mr. Richardson's expertise and experience.'

'The compensation committee being?'

'A subcommittee of the board.'

'Would it be fair to say,' Marshall's pacing gathered enthusiasm, 'that a CEO is in a position to reward the members of the board in various ways?'

'I suppose-'

'And they accepted your report?'

'Yes.'

'Can you tell the court what the suggested range was?'

'I don't recall the exact figures, but I remember the committee went with the upper end.'

Hugh felt his lips curl upward. At last, things were going his way. How could it be anything but a glowing endorsement of his worth for the committee to agree to pay him more than they had to? After all, the board never voted to increase anyone else's pay. It wasn't like they just forked over cash indiscriminately.

'Is that unusual?' Marshall's brow furrowed in that special way Hugh knew it did when he was pretending to be confused. He'd used that exact expression dozens of times during Hugh's previous trials, feigning bafflement when Bambi had claimed she deserved half of their assets, or utter bewilderment when he was accused of propositioning his former secretary.

'Not at all,' Jana smiled. 'Most boards opt to pay their CEOs somewhat above the average going rate.'

Marshall's furrowing deepened. 'But isn't the board tasked with looking after shareholders' money? Protecting the nest eggs of the hardworking people who choose to invest in the company?'

Hugh nearly snorted out loud. Even he knew that the vast majority of capital came from individuals and families who were far from 'hardworking', and the only investors who did work hard were those whose pension funds invested in CGM. They hardly had any choice in the matter.

'A CEO's compensation package is one of the most reported statistics about a company's leader. In fact, it is often considered a measure of their performance in and of itself.'

Marshall paced up and down, his face almost comical in its mock-confused contortions by this point. 'Isn't that a bit like saying that the measure of winning a race is collecting the most ribbons – regardless of whether you run the fastest?'

'No board – and presumably no shareholder – wants their CEO to be considered among the bottom of the pack. Offering a CEO an above-average compensation package is a way of signaling to both current and potential investors that the board is confident in their selection. In fact, it is not uncommon for boards to offer even more than the top of the recommended range, just to show how highly they think of their chosen candidate.'

'Confident. You've used that term several times. Can you explain how the system you've just described is any different to a confidence trick? That's why it's called a con job, isn't it? Because they're about instilling confidence in unsuspecting punters.'

'If a CEO is successful – and most research suggests a certain level of confidence is necessary for success – then the shareholders will be successful, too. Yes, CEOs are paid a lot, but shareholders reap the rewards, too.'

'But the CEO is the only one guaranteed to reap the rewards, aren't they? The investors must wait and see whether the CEO's performance can actually live up to the astronomical sum they are paid.'

'Any investor who is unhappy with a CEO's performance can have their voice heard at a shareholder's meeting – or, in the ultimate vote of no confidence, they can sell their shares.'

'They can sell their shares,' Marshall repeated. 'When they realize the emperor has no clothes, so to speak, investors can sell their shares – hoping they get out before anyone else realizes, and their value plummets to zero. The stock market has always privileged the already wealthy. After all, they have more money, and more money means more 'votes', as you put it. But isn't it true, Ms. Dryser, that the vast majority of buying and selling these days is undertaken by computers, rather than people? That algorithms are making these decisions, not humans? That the stock market is sharply divided into two classes: those who have access to powerful computers and software which allow them to make millions in milliseconds, by buying or selling instants before others are able to, and those who have to rely on their own wits and accessible technology?'

Hugh willed Jana to say something, but she remained silent. Marshall hadn't really asked her a question – he was just up there pontificating. He looked across to Joseph, who seemed to be preoccupied picking something out of his teeth.

'So once you've made your recommendations,' Marshall continued, 'and the board has decided upon a rate of remuneration, what happens next?'

Jana smiled the sort of tight-lipped grimace one might put on when climbing back on the horse that has just bucked you off. 'The proposed package will go to a shareholder's vote.'

'And I imagine the shareholders normally object to these enormous raises?'

'On the contrary, the vast majority of packages are approved. Indeed, Many firms believe that compensating a CEO well, especially through stockholdings, aids in aligning the CEO's values with those of the owners.'

'Is this same approach taken when it comes to other members of staff? Are those workers who don't demonstrate alignment with the company's values and strategic interests given enormous cash bonuses to persuade them in the right direction?'

'There are other ways to persuade lower-level staff.'

'Such as? Monitoring their performance? Dismissing them?'

Joseph dragged his attention away from the stains on his tie long enough to lodge another objection, before Marshall came in for one last stab.

'Ms. Dryser, how is it that you became acquainted with Mr. Richardson?'

'I was consulting at Hardings, and Mr. Richardson is a member of the board there. I have provided compensation consulting services for both Hardings and CGM for a number of years now.'

'How interesting. Mr. Harding is a member of CGM's board, and Mr. Richardson is a member of the Hardings board.'

'Yes. That is hardly unusual.'

'Who was it that engaged your services for CGM initially?'

'The board.'

'Which member of the board specifically?'

'Mr. Harding.'

'I see. A close family friend of Mr. Richardson. Did anyone else consult on this matter?'

'Yes – a team of lawyers was engaged to assess the legality of the offer, and several investment banks provided feedback on the package's acceptability to investors.'

'And these consultants were hired by an unbiased, external, third-party?'

'I believe they were also hired by the board.'

'Do you know which member of the board specifically?'

'Mr. Harding.'

'And you recommended an increase for Mr. Harding at his company, too, I presume?'

'Yes.'

'And the board, including Mr. Richardson, approved of Mr. Harding's raise, just as the board of CGM, including Mr. Harding, approved of Mr. Richardson's raise?'

'Yes.'

'And then the shareholders of their respective companies approved their raises?'

'No.'

'Sorry?'

Jana leaned closer to the microphone. 'No. The shareholders voted against Mr. Harding's raise.'

'And yet Mr. Richardson specifically requested the consultation committee at CGM employ your services.'

'Well, Mr. Harding's raise was approved in the end.'

'Now, I'm confused,' Marshall flashed his furrowed brow again. 'Who approves of the package if the shareholders have voted against it?'

'The board. A shareholders' vote is often non-binding.'

'I see. The board approves of it anyway.'

There was a pause. Hugh willed him to end it there – not least because he was desperate for a piss. But Marshall hadn't become Hugh's go-to lawyer by leaving good enough alone. He didn't just kill his prey, he dragged their lifeless bodies around afterwards.

'Ms. Dryser, you mentioned that your role is 'cyclical'. What does this entail?'

'Well, the evaluation of CEO compensation is cyclical, so compensation consultancy has to be, too.'

'Your services are frequently re-engaged?'

'Correct. I provide my consultancy to companies on an annual basis.'

'How does that process work?'

Jana took a sip of water, leaving a crescent of pink lipstick on the glass. 'In subsequent years, I would again provide the committee with data on the compensation packages of comparable CEOs, and give a recommended range.'

'Is this recommendation typically more, less, or about the same as the previous year's?'

'Given the rise in compensation among other CEOs, the rate would typically increase, in order to remain competitive.'

'Ms. Dryser, I have here a chart of Mr. Richardson's base pay over his tenure as CEO. The same data evaluated by the AutoAutomator software produced by my client. Could you describe for me what trends you, as an experienced compensation consultant, see in this graph?'

Jana took the paper from Marshall. A copy was projected on the screen. Hugh didn't even need to look to know what it showed: up, up, up. He had that graph seared into his memory, like a brand on a steak.

'Mr. Richardson's base pay appears to have remained relatively stable, before increasing in recent years.'

Most of those increases, Hugh knew, were in large part thanks to Jana's efforts.

'Here,' Marshall pointed theatrically, 'There is a sharp increase, is there not? An almost doubling of pay. Can you explain how Mr. Richardson's experience and expertise altered to warrant such a dramatic raise?'

'That particular year,' Jana looked down at her own notes, 'a number of similar companies increased their CEO's base salary, and the board of CGM felt it prudent to follow suit, in order to retain Mr. Richardson's services.'

'Isn't it awfully coincidental, though, that this increase in base salary occurred when the loophole permitting unlimited tax deductions for stocks and options was closed?'

Jana fixed Marshall with a steely glare. Hugh had never seen her so combative.

'It is no coincidence. As there was no longer a tax benefit associated with offering CEOs a larger portion of their compensation package in the form of stocks and options, many companies opted for increasing their CEO's base pay instead.'

'So this change was not associated with a change in CEO performance?'

'As I mentioned, compensation consulting is not merely – or even primarily – about evaluating a CEO's capacities and performance, but about assessing the market. And as the market changed, Mr. Richardson's compensation changed too. Companies are obligated to pay CEOs competitive rates if they don't want the best talent to be snapped up by firms overseas. There is a fierce global market for outstanding leadership.'

'Ms. Dryser, you have testified that you provide consulting services to a number of the largest corporations in the nation. How many of them have CEOs recruited from abroad?'

'I'm not sure there are any-'

'And in your more than a decade of experience, how many CEOs have been poached by foreign companies and enticed overseas?'

'Well, none that I know of.'

'Ms. Dryser, isn't it true that when it comes to a 'fierce global market', we're not really talking about the C-suite? ToyStar, for example, has an entirely local board – Mr. Richardson is one of the members – and yet all of their factories are based overseas.'

'Relevance!' Joseph objected, as if waking from a fever dream. The sweat on Joseph's brow – and staining of the armpits of his suit – made Hugh suspect he really might have.

Marshall waved a dismissive apology. 'Let me see if I have this right: you provide consultation services to companies like Hardings, which almost always select an above-average compensation package, thereby lifting the average pay of CEOs in the field. You then perform similar consulting services for other board members, such as Mr. Richardson, using this newly increased average, and his board likewise approves an above-average compensation package for him.'

'Typically, yes.'

'And then, once you or your colleagues have provided services for all those other CEOs, with ever-increasing recommendations, I suppose it's time to re-evaluate Mr. Harding's pay. And then Mr. Richardson's. And so on. At even higher rates than before.'

'It is important to maintain industry standards.'

'Has there ever been a year in which you have recommended a CEO receive a decrease in pay?'

'Not that I recall.'

'Even when CGM reported losses of $80 million and Mr. Richardson fired 5,000 employees?'

'My role is to provide recommendations on the basis of the market rate, not Mr. Richardson's performance.'

'No further questions.'

CHAPTER 15

Hugh was buzzing. He couldn't tell whether it was the case, the caffeine, or the indignity of having to drink out of a paper cup in the courthouse cafeteria. But he felt ready to face another day.

'Mr. Rich, can you describe your job for us please?'

'I'm a talent scientist at TalentX,' Chad Rich smiled, his dazzling teeth as captivating as his designer stubble. Hugh wished he could get his own facial hair to look like that, but his grew in bushy on one side and patchy on the other. The man looked more like a personal trainer than a scientist – and Hugh ought to know. His first wife had run off on him with her trainer.

'I advise companies on how they can better attract, retain, and promote talented individuals, with a special focus on C-suite executives, in addition to my work with professional athletes.'

Hugh could see why Jana had recommended this guy. He was brilliant. Hugh already felt convinced of whatever Chad was going to say, and he hadn't even gotten into the meat of his testimony yet.

'What experience do you have in this field?'

'In addition to consulting for several of the largest firms in the country, I was invited to give a guest lecture at Hardville College.'

'And as a talent scientist, Mr. Rich, how do you define talent?'

'There are many observable behaviors common to all successful leaders. They are competitive, dedicated to continuous improvement. They work long hours, hate whining, know where they want to go, and make decisions.'

Joseph brushed the greasy strand of hair covering his forehead aside. 'What other remarkable characteristics do these CEOs have?'

Chad's face lit up. 'It's undeniable that they have a certain presence. They look the part, and most CEOs have the ability to command a room. They manage by the numbers, but don't lead by them, instead, focusing on human elements. And most important of all, they aren't afraid to make mistakes.'

Take that! Hugh nodded to himself. That Mike J. Guy wouldn't know a human element if it slapped him in the face or threw a drink at him.

If there was one thing Hugh did, that was it. Make mistakes.

'A CEO is a talented individual, and any discussion of their value must take this talent into account. Consider athletes, musicians, lawyers, or plastic surgeons. They all form part of a team. Sports teams are the obvious analogy. But even athletes in individual events rely on a team of doctors and coaches and other personnel.'

'Go on.'

'Music stars rely on the members of their band or orchestra, or on backup vocalists or dancers. And even individual performers draw on songwriters and managers and crew. A surgeon has doctors to make diagnoses. Assistants to pass them implements during surgery. Nursing staff to care for patients in recovery. You yourself as a lawyer would have a team of paralegals to help prepare documents and file motions.'

Hugh snorted. He couldn't imagine Joseph having employing the services of even a single paralegal, let alone a whole team.

'All these people are highly trained and hardworking. Yet, it is talent that the market rewards. Those who stand head and shoulders above the rest in their field. The exceptional ones. Like specialists in all fields, CEOs attract high pay for three reasons. To compensate them for the investments they have made prior to their employment. For the dangerous conditions they encounter during their employment. And for their projected employability post-retirement.'

'Are there any other universal traits of CEOs?'

'CEOs are great at multitasking. Unfortunately, their attention span is often misunderstood as a lack of caring or empathy.'

'Isn't that a problem? If CEOs, the figureheads of a company, are perceived as uncaring?'

'Not necessarily.' The words rolled off Chad's well-rehearsed tongue. 'I recently wrote an article titled "*Why You Shouldn't Hire a Nice CEO*".'

'Can you give us a summary?'

'A study of over 2,000 CEOs found that a CEO's decisiveness is more important in determining their performance than how nice they are.'

'What exactly do you mean by "nice"?'

'A "nice" CEO might stretch their team across too many priorities because they struggle to say no to anyone. They might allow weak players to hold the company back, because they don't want to fire anyone. Tolerate mediocrity for longer than they should. And by avoiding conflict, they end up not giving critical feedback when it is most needed. By contrast, a CEO considered unempathetic or uncaring might actually be an asset.'

For a moment, Hugh wondered whether they could get Bambi on the stand as a last-minute surprise witness. She'd have no trouble testifying that Hugh was unempathetic and uncaring.

Then Marshall approached. Swishing around in his suit that must have cost more than Joseph's house, the shininess of his shoes even out-glimmering Chad's teeth.

'Mr. Rich, you view CEOs as similar to professional athletes?'

'Yes, I think that's a good analogy.'

'Isn't it true though, that athletes on a team earn similar amounts?'

'As in business, exceptional players are rewarded with exceptional salaries. Particularly good players are offered more lucrative deals by rival teams. This means those talented players must be adequately rewarded in order for their home teams to retain them. The same is true of particularly talented CEOs.'

'So, we would see similar wage gaps in sporting teams as in corporate teams? With one player earning several hundred, even several thousand times what his teammates do?'

'Well, no. But I don't think it's fair to describe CEOs and their lowest level employees as playing on the same team. CEOs, if you'll pardon the analogy, are in a different league altogether.'

'That's not what the plaintiffs have said though, is it? I quote Mr. Park's latest PearShape product release statement: "We couldn't have made this happen without the entire team". And Mr. Richardson's letter to his shareholders last year: "At CGM, we play as a team. Every player is vital to the success of our business."'

Hugh had always dreamed of hearing one of his letters read aloud by a learned man to a room full of eager listeners. Especially by someone with a voice as resonant and commanding as Marshall's.

He only wished his own words were not being used as evidence against him.

'Clearly,' Chad waved a hand, 'those statements are little more than puff. Marketing bluster. They're not meant to be taken seriously.'

'I have more,' Marshall shook a pile of papers.

Hugh had always felt reassured by the vast trolleys of papers his lawyers wheeled back and forth between court cases. He couldn't imagine they, or indeed anyone, had read all of them. In fact, he half suspected they were blank reams. But they made for a good show.

Now, he was sickly aware that his words had at last been collected and poured over, and it wasn't good.

'The majority of these statements,' Marshall continued, 'are collected from official internal memos. Employee handbooks. The minutes of shareholder's meetings. Are we to treat information delivered by the CEO in these sorts of venues as "marketing bluster"?'

'To some extent, anything a CEO says serves as a form of marketing. That's why they're so valuable to companies-'

'Continuing with your analogy, Mr. Rich, you proposed that part of the reason CEOs earn so much is to compensate them for the investments they have made in the past. Can you please describe how much the average CEO forks out of their own pocket prior to taking on the role?'

Chad coughed. 'It's more of an investment in themselves than in the company. Much as a professional athlete spends years training to perform at their peak. Many of the largest companies today are knowledge-based firms in high-tech industries which require highly-specialized talent to lead them.'

'Can you explain for us the prerequisite training involved in becoming a CEO?'

'Most CEOs have a college degree of some variety.'

'How is that different to many of their employees? Engineers at Mr. Park's company, for example, must hold a degree in engineering. According to the Harding's handbook, accountants at Mr. Harding's investment firm must possess a degree in accounting from an accredited school of business and economics. What is the required training for someone to be considered CEO of such high-tech or high-knowledge firms?'

'It's a mixture of formal and informal experience.'

'In other words, there is none?'

'I wouldn't put it like that. It's a complex fusion, a mélange of-'

'Yes or no, Mr. Rich. Is there a required, recognized form of formal training for someone to be considered a CEO?'

'No.'

'That's in rather stark contrast to the other occupations you mentioned though, isn't it? Musicians and athletes undertake years of dedicated training before they can earn large sums. Or even, before they begin to earn anything at all!'

Marshall paused for emphasis. Hugh thought he could spy a few long-haired idiots nodding, themselves likely frustrated artists.

'The vast majority play as a hobby, as amateurs. Only a select few – often those who began training as young children – rise to the level where they can make a career of it. And their careers are often limited. Singers lose their voices or their popularity. Athletes suffer joint and brain damage that not only prevent long-term sporting careers, and impact their enjoyment of life in the short- and long-term, but even impede their post-play employment in other fields. Isn't that right?'

'Objection! We're not here to examine the careers of celebrities, sporting or otherwise,' Joseph interjected. Hugh felt wounded – wasn't he a celebrity? Wasn't that what Joseph had said back in his dingy little office?

'Sustained' Joseph grinned like he'd scored a point.

'Mr. Rich,' Marshall stared so hard, Hugh was certain he could see Chad's designer stubble tremble on his chiseled chin. 'What was the name of the seminar you gave at Hardville College last year?'

Chad mumbled something.

'I'm sorry, could you repeat for the benefit of those of us without exceptional hearing?'

'"Financial management for athletes: Planning beyond the lifespan of your knees."'

'Surely this is irrelevant!'

'On the contrary,' Marshall declared. 'Key features of the careers of singers and sports stars – and indeed surgeons – are that first, they require many years of training. And second, the span of most is limited by the physical limitations of the human body. It is not unreasonable for players to be rewarded for undertaking activities which their employers know, with a high degree of certainty, will be responsible for injuring, even killing them. That is the true meaning of compensation. To make whole a loss – such as the loss of employability many professional athletes face once their skulls are crushed, their knees pulverized. Just as there is an allowance for danger built into the contracts of armed forces personnel and war reporters, and those who scale high buildings to wash windows, it makes sense for athletes to be compensated for the dangers of their job. That they be provided with an income that should set them up for the future. Likewise, it is reasonable that surgeons, who spend years in training, not only foregoing income, but incurring large amounts of debt as they do so, be made whole for this loss they have suffered prior to becoming surgeons.'

'As I said, the majority of CEOs do hold degrees.'

'Mr. Rich, no one is surprised that I, as a lawyer, earn more than, say, a McKing's grill operator, or one of the workers at Ms. Frost or Mr. Park's factories.'

'True. Those positions do not require the same level of professional training.'

'And yet you have testified that there is no required training of CEOs, correct.'

'Well, not strictly. But as I said, the majority of CEOs do bring considerable training to the table.'

'Mr. Kim, the CEO of one of the biggest tech firms on the planet, holds a certificate in real estate investing. Mr. Jefferson attended two semesters at his father's alma mater, thanks to their children of alumni acceptance policy. Ms. Frost majored in ancient irrigation systems. Mr. Harding earned a degree from a for-profit university before it was revealed he paid someone else to take his exams. Mr. Richardson began a degree in liberal arts, majoring in wine appreciation, which he dropped out of. Would you consider these degrees relevant to their positions?'

'The plaintiffs represent a wealth of experience in broad fields, as you have illustrated.'

'Your view is that their pay should take into account this "wealth of experience" regardless of the field of their training?'

'Indeed.'

'Mr. Rich, what do you think would be the chances of me obtaining a job at one of Mr. Jefferson's laboratories? Say, as a research chemist?'

'Unless you have a PhD in chemistry as well as law, I'd say the chances are pretty slim. You'd have more luck in the legal department.'

'Mr. Rich, were I to get a job in one of Mr. Park or Ms. Frost's factories, would my pay take into account the wealth of experience I have in practicing law?'

'I wouldn't think so. It wouldn't be pertinent to the position.'

'And yet you believe that Mr. Richardson deserves to be paid $58 million a year because he knows how to identify a good red? Is that pertinent to the position? Does CGM produce a lot of wine?'

'I'm not sure that CGM produces anything.'

'Yet you believe you are in a position to assess Mr. Richardson's talent? Without even an inkling of what his business does?'

Hugh crossed his arms over his chest. Marshall was like a rabid dog with a bone. His questions were so unfair! It wasn't as if Hugh knew what all of CGM's subsidiaries did –and he was the CEO! So how could Chad be expected to know?

'If investing in one's education is so vital to acting as a CEO that it is deserving of added compensation, we should see a marked difference in the performance between those CEOs with degrees versus those without . And if boards viewed CEO's education as vital, we should also see a clear difference between the salaries of those CEOs with degrees versus those without. Is there such a difference, Mr. Rich?'

'Not to my knowledge.'

For a brief moment, Hugh thought it was all over, as Marshall returned to his table. But then, energy restored by a sip of water, the man burst out into questions once more.

'Mr. Rich, what is the average career span of a professional athlete? Would you say it is longer, or shorter, than that of a CEO?'

'I couldn't say.'

'You couldn't say? Isn't it true that many CEOs work until they are in their seventies or older?'

'Yes, but it varies depending on the individual-'

'Of all the board positions across the top 500 companies in this country, just 2% are held by people under the age of 45. In fact, there are more directors over the age of 75 than there are under 50! Would it be fair to say that you have a number of clients in their seventies, including Mr. Jefferson here?'

'Yes, but-'

'And how many professional athletes in their 70s do you represent?'

'Well, none. But CEOs aren't the only ones to work until the age of 70. Many of the employees at Mr. Jefferson's company are post the typical retirement age. PharmaX has an excellent record for retaining senior workers. And in fact,' Chad showed off the full range of his teeth, 'Hardings Bank recently made the news when one of its most senior employees passed away, at the age of ninety-eight.'

Hugh remembered that article. Hardings had been in a mad rush to brainstorm how they could capitalize on the nonagenarian's death. They'd been hoping he'd hold out to 100.

'Yet according to recent PharmaX employee satisfaction surveys, senior workers are not continuing to work because they want to. Or because they feel valued by the company. Rather, the low wages and few benefits they have received in previous decades mean they haven't got enough to retire. Even middle management who invested their savings in the company lost out in the financial crisis, and can no longer afford to retire. A crisis engineered by firms such as Hardings.'

'Investing carries inherent risks.'

'Are those the sort of risks you referred to when you mentioned the "dangers" of the job?'

'Yes. There are psychological dangers – serving as a CEO is a stressful position. But also, as you have highlighted, financial risks. One of the main reasons CEOs are paid a large proportion of their income in stocks is so that they have some "skin in the game" to use another sporting analogy.'

Hugh approved of all these sports references. He didn't know much about sports – the closest he ever got was driving a sports car. And a few failed attempts at football and fencing at St. Lucre's. But he always bought season tickets to all the major sporting events for the same reason he suspected Chad was talking about sports now – because it made him seem more relatable, and perhaps, even heroic by association.

'The CEO might be a team player, but he – or she,' Chad corrected himself – is a very special player. The Most Valuable Player, if you will. The one fans pack the stands to see.'

'But Mr. Rich, how many patients buy Mr. Jefferson's drugs because of his fame as the CEO? How many children ask for a GI John doll out of admiration for Ms. Frost?'

'Not many, I suppose.'

'Mr. Rich, you mentioned the psychological stress involved in a CEO's position. Can you please elaborate?'

'CEOs are responsible not only for supporting themselves and their own family members. They are responsible for the livelihoods of all their workers. This added responsibility is an immense burden upon the CEO's psyche.'

Hugh did his best to look burdened by responsibility, in case anyone was looking.

'Wouldn't you say that CEOs could eliminate much of that worry by taking a pay cut? If, for example, a CEO such as Ms. Frost earns as much as 5,000 of her employees, that is, an entire quarter of her manufacturing force put together, couldn't she accept a pay cut that would guarantee the livelihoods of a large proportion of her workforce? That would seem to be a very simple decision – yet one that none of the CEOs at this table have undertaken.'

'It's not simply the stress of being responsible for one's employees' income,' Chad frowned. 'CEOs are also held responsible for the income of tens of thousands of investors. And the enjoyment or benefit, and of course, safety, of millions of customers.'

'Is that burden any more stressful than that of, say, a doctor, whose daily practice may involve dozens of literally life-or-death decisions? Or a general who might not only have to manage a large troop, but decide what level of mortal danger they are willing to subject those under their command to?'

Chad frowned. 'Being a CEO is far more than a nine-to-five job. A CEO thinks about the company all the time. When they're at home. With loved ones. It's a 24-hour-a-day, seven-days-a-week commitment.'

'I'm sure your clients sleep on occasion,' Marshall winked. 'But please explain, Mr. Rich, how this is any different to employees who worry about their jobs? Not only do employees worry about the business outside of business hours. They are virtually forced to do so by their superiors. Isn't it true that last year, Mr. Harding, Mr. Jefferson and Mr. Richardson's companies were outed for expecting workers to be constantly available via telephone and email? Asking them to take video conference meetings with clients while they make their kids' breakfast? Come in to shifts at only a few minutes notice, or having their shifts – and their income – canceled with as little notice?'

'I'm not privy to all the business decisions of my clients-'

'In some countries, Mr. Rich, the government has taken steps to ban employers from emailing employees after hours. And then there's the biggest concern of all: what if I get fired? Not only are employees concerned about doing their jobs well, and hopefully progressing through promotions and advancing in their career. They are also concerned about what will happen if they lose their jobs.'

'We worry about that, too!' Hugh interjected. To be fair, he hadn't ever worried about losing his job until the day he opened up the annual report and found his photograph and name were missing. But, he thought, as he tuned out the sound of the banging gavel, he'd certainly thought a lot about it since.

'There's a difference, isn't there, Mr. Rich?' Marshall said, though Hugh knew he was really addressing him. 'Someone in Mr. Richardson's financial position, who has benefited from years of a very high salary. From enormous gifts of stock, and from the financial advice provided free-of-charge to high net-worth individuals. He doesn't have to worry about how he will feed himself, or his children, or repair his car. On the other hand, one of Mr. Richardson's employees, who has been able to pay little into their social security, and who hasn't been able to afford to invest. Who cannot afford financial advice from anyone other than the scam artists who provide biased advice in exchange for huge commissions from the likes of Mr. Harding here... wouldn't it be fair to say that they will have more worries?'

'Different worries,' Chad conceded. 'The fact remains that the role of CEO is a difficult one. One which will impact one's relationships with others – family, existing friendships. And CEOs are often

140

publicly hated. Especially when they have to make unpopular decisions to ensure the continuing success of the company.'

Hugh knew all about that. He swore he could still see marks on his leg from those cardboard chainsaws.

'What sorts of unpopular decisions?'

'The most unpopular – and yet, often most important – decision relates to downsizing.'

'I can see how that would be unpopular. But why important?'

'Downsizing is widely regarded as the preferred method to help declining organizations, by cutting unnecessary costs. The decision to downsize is always a difficult one.'

'Is that why Mr. Harding here was personally rewarded with an eight million dollar bonus for downsizing the workforce of Harding's?'

Chad cleared his throat. 'Mr. Harding's compensation reflects the difficulty of the decisions his position is encumbered with.'

'I don't doubt that there are some very difficult decisions CEOs have to make.'

Hugh was thrilled to see Marshall concede a point.

'But are they any harder than a small business owner faces when they must fire even one employee they know personally? Imagine living in a small community where not only do you have to deal with everyone knowing you fired your sole employee – which makes you look like a failure as a business owner – but you may have to face bumping into your former employee, or their partner, or their kids, at the supermarket, or your child's school. Do any of your clients live in the same neighborhoods as their employees, Mr. Rich? Shop in the same stores? Send their children to the same schools?'

'I wouldn't know-'

'Mr. Rich, I put it to you that CEOs, including those gathered here, tend to be both socioeconomically and geographically distant from their employees. There's almost no chance of Mr. Richardson here bumping into one of his now unemployed workers at his golf club. Or Mr. Harding having an awkward encounter with one of his former clerks at one of the top restaurants he frequents. Even if they were, by some strange coincidence, to meet, it is highly unlikely that either gentleman would be recognized by their former employees. And virtually impossible that either would recognize their former workers. A CEO of a large firm may not be thanked by their employees or even the public at large for thinning the herd. But, as we've seen in the case of Mr. Harding here, they are often richly rewarded for making decisions that impact thousands of people's lives, with raises of millions.'

'It is a demanding job in many respects.'

'Mr. Rich, you characterized CEOs as working long hours, hating whining, knowing where they want to go, and making decisions, correct?'

'That's right.'

'Many of those traits can be observed at all levels of employment, wouldn't you say? What is it that makes a CEO special?'

Chad straightened his back and flashed a smile, his muscular arms straining against the fabric of his shirtsleeves in a way that only Hugh's stomach challenged his clothing.

'While it is true these traits can be found, to a certain extent, across the human spectrum, strong leaders, and CEOs in particular, love making decisions, and are able to do so on the basis of very limited information.'

'Most people enjoy making decisions and having some form of control over their lives. But when they do so on the basis of limited information, isn't that normally characterized as irresponsible or irrational?'

'The nature of the fast-paced and ever-changing corporate environment often prevents careful consideration. Frequently, opportunities are time-sensitive. A quick decision is often better than a well-considered one.'

'Such as the decision to initiate the immediate rollout of a software program designed to automate all jobs that cannot be more profitably and more reliably performed by a machine, without first checking to see whether it would make one's own position redundant? Would you characterize that as a decision which benefited the company by being made in a timely fashion, rather than well thought through?'

The nylon tie around Hugh's neck felt like a noose.

'That particular decision is perhaps an example of how a CEO's decisions are not always self-serving, but can actually be self-sacrificing.'

Hugh breathed a sigh of relief. Yes! That's what he was! A martyr! A victim of his own selflessness! A devoted company man!

'Yet the litigants in this particular case,' Marshall paused to gesture towards Hugh and the rest of the board, 'have claimed – in retrospect, mind you – they were given insufficient information and time to make an informed decision about the implementation of my client's AutoAutomator software.'

Chad squirmed. 'Perhaps we can view this decision as demonstrating that even decisions based on limited information can be in the best interests of the company.'

'So you would characterize the automation of their positions as in the best interests of the company?'

'Look, most CEOs are careful managers, often expressing regret at not taking action when it comes to poor performers sooner.'

'Poor performers like themselves?'

'Stop badgering the witness!'

'CEOs are capable of sizing up teams quickly-'

'That's hardly surprising,' Marshall shot back, 'given they are teams they have assembled themselves, full of their own cronies!'

'You have been warned!'

'Sorry, Mr. Rich, do go on.'

'CEOs ask a lot of great questions, and are extremely intelligent.'

'Mr. Rich, you have a great list of traits here, but may I ask what methodology your claims are based upon? You suggest, for instance, that CEOs are extremely intelligent, but by what measure?'

'IQ tests would be one measure.'

Hugh groaned inwardly. At least, he hoped it was only an inward groan. Joe Joseph had warned him that the opposition might try to throw out IQ-based testimony on the basis that it had been shown to be culturally and linguistically biased, whatever that meant.

But Marshall made no remark disparaging IQ tests at all. He made no move to strike Chad's testimony from the record. Still, Hugh's relief was short lived, his stomach turning to jelly as Marshall's questioning continued:

'Statistics show that the most intelligent people, as measured by IQ tests, are often far from the biggest earners. Is that not correct'

Chad smiled. 'Some might say they are smart enough to have figured out there is more to life than money!'

Nobody laughed, least of all Hugh.

'I'm glad you mention money,' Marshall pondered aloud. 'The average CEO of a large corporation earns 400 times more than their typical employee.' He paused. 'Are we to believe they are 400 times more intelligent?'

'I'm sure we can agree it's not very fair to compare an experienced CEO's salary with that of a minimum wage worker just starting out in their career...'

'You misunderstand, Mr. Rich. The comparison is between CEOs and their average employees, not their lowest-paid employees. The average CEO makes around 800 times more than the minimum wage earner – more than half of whom are over the age of 25. Would you describe that as "staring out"?'

'Objection,' Joseph finally managed to stammer. 'Mr. Rich is not here as an expert on what minimum wage workers earn.'

'But he is here as an expert on what CEOs deserve to earn. A question, I propose, which can only be answered by reference to the incomes of others.'

'Mr. Marshall, please return to the topic at hand.'

'Yes, your honor. Mr. Rich, you have characterized CEOs as "extremely intelligent" - let's set a baseline, shall we? According to the research I have here, most college graduates have an IQ between 104 and 110. Marginally higher than the typical clerical or sales worker, and slightly higher than an average high school graduate. Those with a MD, JD, or PhD tend to have an IQ of around 125. Is that the sort of range we are looking at for CEOs?'

'Well, the typical manager or administrator might have an IQ of about 104.'

'That's a fairly normal score though, isn't it? An IQ of 90 to 109 is considered "average" by most measures. Superior is classed as 110-119, very superior as 120-139, and a genius would have an IQ of over

140 by most measures. The vast bulk of the world's population falls somewhere between 70 and 130 points. I could perhaps understand, Mr. Rich, why boards feel the need to pay so much to attract CEOs if the required IQ is 140, and the pool of possible applicants suitably tiny. Is that the range we are looking at for CEOs?'

'I'm not sure of the exact figures...'

'According to an article by Professor Fennick only 39% of CEOs in the top 500 companies would be considered gifted. I can only assume the proportion would be even lower if we consider CEOs at smaller, less successful firms. In other words, the majority are still within the normal zone. Given the colossal mistakes some CEOs make, costing their companies millions, even billions of dollars, it would seem high intelligence is far from a prerequisite to becoming a CEO, wouldn't you say?'

'I'm not sure.'

'And yet, you consider being unafraid of making mistakes one of the key features of a remarkable CEO?'

'Well, yes-'

'I suppose it's much easier to make mistakes with other people's money, and other people's jobs, isn't it?'

'Objection!'

Marshall held up his hands before brandishing a piece of paper.

'Mr. Rich, could you please identify this document?'

'It would appear to be an article.'

'Commissioned by?'

'TalentX,' Chad swallowed.

'Your firm, in other words. Could you please read the third line of the eighth paragraph for me?'

'The average IQ of the CEOs surveyed was 104 points.'

'One hundred and four? Not one hundred and forty?'

Hugh could almost feel his blood pressure rising. He'd enjoyed watching Marshall's antics when he was on the other side of the courtroom. Seated safely alongside him. The great lawyer striding out to defend him.

Sitting here, on the other side, Marshall's barbs felt nasty – cheap attacks dressed up in an expensive suit and aftershave.

'One hundred and four,' Chad confirmed.

'One hundred and four!' Marshall exclaimed with rhetorical flourish. 'No different to the typical manager, who is paid just a tiny fraction of what the CEO receives. Mr. Rich, is it not true that, if the average CEO's IQ is 104 points, and almost 40% of CEOs of the top 500 companies are "gifted", that there must be an awful lot of CEOs with below-average intelligence running firms?'

'That is how percentages and averages work,' Chad cleared his throat. 'But it's worth mentioning the fact that 59% of the female CEOs who were tested for that article were ranked as "highly gifted". The average female CEO, if memory serves, has an IQ of about 131 points.'

Hugh eyed Deborah with a mixture of disbelief that she could possibly be smarter than him, and gratitude that finally, her token addition to the group was paying off.

'I'm sure we can agree, Mr. Rich, that this disparity has more to do with discrimination against women than any innate intellectual superiority among women. The average female CEO may be smarter than the average male CEO, but only because boards are so biased against women they have to be smarter than a similarly qualified man in order to be selected.'

Hugh scoffed indignantly. He wasn't sure which was more ludicrous. The suggestion that the board was biased, or the suggestion that Deborah was smarter than him.

'What you have told us, Mr. Rich, amounts to CEOs having average, or perhaps ever-so-slightly above average intelligence. In fact, these figures suggest the average CEO has an IQ below the level we'd expect for someone of their education and employment.'

'Well,' Chad coughed. 'There is some evidence to suggest that having a very high IQ can actually present a problem when it comes to high-level management. CEOs with high IQs are often seen as poor listeners, and even perceived as resentful of having to explain their decisions to staff.'

'Which is it Mr. Rich? Are good CEOs, as you put it, "extremely intelligent"? Or does high intelligence make for a poor CEO?'

'I suppose you could say that, like most things in life, balance is necessary. Not too smart, not too dull. The Goldilocks principle, if you will.'

Hugh could almost feel himself nodding along. For all that Marshall had thrown at him, Chad had handled that masterfully.

'In other words, CEOs are of average intelligence – as your IQ survey seems to suggest.'

'A good mix of qualities is more important than simply being smart. Knowing the right people, being able to talk the talk...'

'That's a rather discouraging message for all those workers who are smarter than their bosses, isn't it? You'll forever be subjected to someone else's inept decision making. Doesn't this lead to backlash, when CEOs are paid so much more than those who are doing the actual work – and who may often be better decision makers too?'

'Again, this is an area in which a talent scientist such as myself can help. Essentially, it's an issue of communication.'

'So your theory, Mr. Rich, is that managing CEO pay is primarily a matter of communication to workers? Rather than ensuring the pay accurately matches the CEO's performance?'

'Yes. But I'd say communication is key in all matters of compensation, not just the CEO's.'

'How so?'

'Studies suggest that more than 80% of employees are happy to be underpaid, so long as their employer effectively communicates the reason for their smaller paycheck. Additionally, research shows mixed outcomes when it comes to pay disparity in organizations. Research supports the idea known as "tournament theory".'

'Tournament theory?'

'As pay differences between levels of roles increase, the value of receiving a promotion rises. This encourages employees to make more of an effort. Where an employee sees the person above them making a lot more money, but they feel as if putting in a little more effort, they could get there too, it makes them much more likely to strive for promotion than if they had to work much harder for only a little reward.'

'Does this extend to the CEO level though? After all, there can only be one CEO.'

'Think of a golf tournament. The more money there is available for golfers to win, the better they tend to play. It's motivating, even if only one person can win the prize.'

'In a golf tournament, everyone who has entered has both a desire and a chance to win. Does this translate to corporate environments? Where the vast majority of employees have little or no chance of ever getting to the top? I mean, in golf, a little competition is healthy. It's a solo sport. But in a corporate environment, competition can be toxic. At the end of the day, aren't employees supposed to be on the same team? Striving together, not bringing one another down?'

'Maybe. But think of the dream the CEO represents! Spend five minutes on any social media platform, and search "CEO life" or "CEO mindset". You'll be bombarded by images of fancy watches and sharp suits, leather chairs and fast cars. All overlaid with inspirational quotes – from people who've probably never met a CEO, let alone been one. People look up to CEOs – to powerful executives in general, really.'

'And in certain segments of the community, people look up to high-up drug dealers. It's what leads them to take risks, selling on street corners for an extremely low cut – a few dollars an hour – in spite of the high risks of dying on the job.'

Chad shifted uneasily. 'I'm not sure the two situations are all that similar...'

'The upper echelons of drug gangs even call themselves 'the board of directors'. You don't need to have experienced corporate life to know something of the inner workings of corporations. After all, there are lots of movies about sharply dressed CEOs and their scandalous investment scams – as well as the social media you mentioned.'

'Maybe there are some similarities. But the fact remains that employees look up to CEOs. They want to be like them. Programmers, lawyers, whatever. They're willing to start at the bottom, pull 80-hour weeks, make a pittance busting their guts for stock options or promotions that never come. So long as they have someone to look up to. An inspirational CEO is worth a huge amount to a company if they can motivate workers to work hard.'

'In essence, you are saying that CEOs do not deserve their pay because they work hard, but because they inspire others to work hard?'

Chad beamed. 'That's it in a nutshell. Imagine if companies had to pay workers for the 80 hours they actually worked instead of the 40 they have on the books. Overnight, payroll costs would double. Not to mention all the fines they'd be paying for violating labor laws if they actually acknowledged how much overtime they require. Sure, it might cost tens of millions to pay a CEO, but if each major corporation had to pay workers what they were really due, it would cost considerably more. It's far cheaper to prop up a celebrity CEO and have everyone working so hard to try and become the next one they don't think about how bad they've got it now.'

'Wouldn't it be reasonable to assume that those workers who are aware of how unlikely it is for them to ever become not just CEO, but an executive of any kind, might be demotivated by this? Research has shown that large pay disparities can also foster resentment. Lower-paid employees become more likely to shrug off their responsibilities or even quit if a better opportunity comes along.'

Chad leaned back in his chair and grunted. 'Equity theory.'

'Would you please enlighten us about this "equity theory"?'

'When employees feel their efforts aren't being rewarded, they're likely to feel resentful.'

'Especially if they see CEOs earning far more than them?'

'Yes. Bad behavior on the part of employees attempting to "get back" at their CEO is not uncommon.'

'And what would you characterize as "bad behavior"?'

'An employee too poor to quit their job may not work as hard. Something characterized as "quiet quitting". Or they might steal office supplies.' Chad's frown of disapproval looked just like Hugh's first ex's personal trainer when he saw Hugh in gym shorts.

Hugh felt his own face taking on the same expression, as he imagined those no-good employees ferreting away pens and rolls of toilet paper they were ill entitled to.

'And what is the value of these paper clips or rolls of tape in comparison to how much companies would have to pay workers if they gave them all they were due?'

'I don't have the exact figures to hand,' Chad sniffed, 'but employee theft is a substantial drain on companies nation-wide.'

'Yet not so substantial that it would be worth paying employees what they are due?'

'I don't know.'

'So what exactly does a CEO do, in your view?'

'One important role is selecting talented individuals to help run the company.'

'Is that how you would describe this diagram?' Marshall asked. He gestured to a glossy illustration of the web of relationships between CGM and the other members' boards.

'I'd say it demonstrates the high levels of mutually recognized talent available in this pool of CEOs.'

'Wouldn't it also be fair to say that it represents a form of – if you'll pardon the expression – ass covering?'

Somehow, words like 'ass' could fall from Marshall's honeyed lips and still sound more refined than whatever came out of Joseph's mouth.

'Evidence of CEOs selecting their friends – or friends of friends – to sit on their board and approve their pay? Who will approve their friends' pay in turn?'

'That's a rather uncharitable interpretation.' Chad frowned. 'But a CEO's role is far broader. They must also represent the company, acting as its public face on a grand scale. The CEO is tasked with representing the company across all media.'

It was Marshall's turn to frown. 'That's a somewhat dated notion, isn't it? Granted, CEOs still feature in the old media – we see their faces on the cover of *Fobbs* or *Top CEO Magazine*; in films, or on television. But Mr. Rich, as you'd know all too well, these media are rapidly losing their audiences.'

'The gentlemen represented in this case have social media profiles, on all the major platforms!'

Marshall's frown turned into an enormous smile which he held for several moments.

'Mr. Rich, I have here a selection of the posts on these platforms. Would you care to read one?'

Chad looked as if he might be sick.

'Go on,' Marshall coaxed.

Chad made the sort of pleading eyes at the judge that FouFou made when she wanted food. 'I don't think I can,' he said.

'Allow me to summarize,' Marshall announced with a flourish, sweeping a glance over at Hugh. Hugh knew exactly what was coming next. 'The first is a message which Mr. Richardson intended to send privately to his secretary, but inadvertently sent to all of the company's followers. How would you rate the value of that post to CGM?'

Sure, his messages were a matter of public record now, but Hugh was relieved Chad had refused to read the post out. It had been bad enough the first time around.

'Indiscretions happen to the best of us,' Chad said. 'But what's important to focus on here isn't the specifics of a particular post, but the online audience Mr. Richardson cultivated over time.'

'Certainly,' Marshall said, peering at the page. 'I believe CGM had a total of 386 followers at the time.'

Hugh remembered that figure all too well. At first, he'd been proud of having so many followers – before he found out that his daughter had three times as many. In fact, Marshall had described the number as 'paltry' and 'insignificant' when attempting to diminish the damage Hugh's sexual escapades had caused the company's public image.

'Would you describe that figure as typical for the CEO of a company of CGM's size?'

'I wouldn't say it's unusual.'

'I think my goddaughter has more followers!' Marshall chuckled. Hugh blistered. Marshall's god-daughter was his daughter. 'What about the next one? Posted by Mr. Hardings?'

'It's a… shopping list,' Chad stumbled.

'Another accidental public post?'

'It would appear so.'

'And what does this *shopping list* have on it?'

Chad cleared his throat. 'A number of… illicit substances.'

'I see. And the next, by Mr. Park? Could you read that one for us verbatim?'

'Women in tech should be thankful they have jobs, not asking for raises.' Chad exhaled, his breath popping against the microphone on the stand.

'Mr. Rich, you've testified that you've worked closely with each of these three gentlemen, to improve their public image. Would you characterize these disclosures as beneficial to their public image?'

'No.'

'What were the outcomes of each of these gaffes?'

'Each of the men involved made an apology, and I recommended the services of a social media team.'

'In other words, these men's accounts were subsequently maintained by junior staff? Many of whom, in turn, outsourced the copywriting, and relied on software to automate posting on behalf of the company. Is that accurate?'

'Yes. For Mr. Richardson, Mr. Hardings, and Mr. Park. I do not believe Ms. Frost or Mr. Jefferson employ such teams.'

'Isn't that because they don't have public social media profiles?

'Well, yes.'

'And is this best practice for CEOs?'

'Best practice differs depending on the field and-'

'Mr. Rich, I have here a copy of an article you wrote in May of last year. Would you care to read the highlighted section?'

Chad sighed again. 'Surveys consistently show that most people believe CEOs should be engaged on social media. 81% of employees believe that CEOs who are online are more equipped to steer a company in the modern world. And 82% of consumers say they are more likely to trust a company when the CEO and other leadership appear accessible and active on social media.' Chad looked up.

'Please continue Mr. Rich.'

'Yet our data shows that less than a third of CEOs actually use social media. And only 4% contribute to blogs, even though blogging has been demonstrated to improve the public perceptions of a CEO.'

'Mr. Rich, how would you characterize the public perception of CEO earnings?'

'I would say there is a level of anger. Tension. But studies show that, generally speaking, people are relatively uninformed about how much executives really make.'

'So your job is to communicate those figures to the public?'

Chad flashed Marshall a pitying smile. 'No.'

'Mr. Rich, when you say that people are generally uninformed about how much executives make, do you mean they overestimate?'

'Underestimate,' Chad coughed.

'Would it be plausible to assume that, if more people were aware just how much the CEOs gathered here earn, they would be even angrier than they already are?'

'I suppose.'

'So why hire you? Why don't CEOs simply pay themselves less?'

'There isn't really a surplus of talented CEOs lining up to be paid less than market rates.'

'What about the evidence that suggests the best paid CEOs are statistically among the worst performers?'

'My job is to help CEOs communicate why they are worth it – not to question whether they are.'

CHAPTER 16

'Please state your name and occupation for the record.'

'Professor Franklin H. Colbert. Tenured professor and PharmaX Harding's Chair of Business at the University of Hardville Nevil G. Stanford School of Business and Economics.'

'Professor, how do you evaluate the effectiveness of a CEO?'

At least Joseph had saved the big gun for last. Even if no one – including Hugh – had been much convinced by the experts he himself had hired once Marshall was finished ripping every last shred of flesh from their bones. Surely, the professor's testimony would be unimpeachable.

He would never have been given a chair sponsored by Hardings and PharmaX if he was anything other than top-notch.

'There are many reliable measures of CEO attributes.'

'Care to elaborate?'

'A CEO's values and reputation are two key measures. We have found that leaders, at all levels, matter to the company. But the more senior a leader is, the more people they impact. A team leader might influence their direct reports. But we would expect a CEO to influence an entire company.'

'And how do they achieve that?'

'Via meetings, and communications to employees. Analyzing the transcripts of meetings between CEOs and other management, it is possible to predict the success or transparency of a company, by evaluating how confident and open a CEO is. A good CEO, as the saying goes, is worth his weight in gold.'

Hugh suppressed a laugh. If that were true, Parker would be worth more than the rest of them put together.

Upon reflection, he probably was.

'It's a common misconception,' the professor continued, 'that paying CEOs less will result in the workers getting more money. But this isn't true. Like CEOs, employees are paid according to what the market says they are worth. If an accountant at Mr. Harding's bank has agreed to work for $30,000 a year, it is because he finds this to be an agreeable arrangement.'

'That sounds reasonable.'

'Sure, he might like to earn more. Wouldn't we all! But if he has accepted a $30,000 position, it is reasonable to assume that he was unable to find a position paying more. There are plenty of others willing to take the job if he does not want it. Or, if he did manage to find a better paying job, but opted not to pursue it, it is reasonable to assume he wasn't willing to put in the time and effort to deal with the increased responsibility a job paying, say, $35,000 a year might entail.'

'Wouldn't it be easy to find plenty of people willing to step into the role of a CEO?' Joseph asked. Hugh noticed that a little of Marshall's rhetorical flourish appeared to have rubbed off on him. 'I imagine there would be quite a few people willing to fill the shoes of any of the gentlemen sitting at this table.'

'There will always be dreamers!' Colbert smiled. 'But just because someone thinks they'd like a job as a CEO or COO or whatever doesn't mean a board would consider them. Most boards, when surveyed, estimate that there are only five or six people in the world who could replace their current CEO!'

'Professor, you mentioned that CEO pay, if reduced, would not be redirected toward employee reimbursement. Why is that?'

'All money in a public company, at the end of the day, belongs not to the employees, or even the CEO, but to the shareholders. Employees shouldn't be upset if a CEO earns too much – but the shareholders should be! Any wage increase comes from their pockets, after all.'

'How can a board know when a CEO is being paid too much? When does a CEO's compensation package cross the line, from attractive to unfair?'

'Whether it is "fair" that a CEO gets paid more than their employees is not a relevant question for the board of directors. The task of any board is to attract and retain stellar talent. So the comparisons the board should be making are in terms of other CEOs' pay, not comparisons to workers' pay. Companies have to offer attractive packages to potential candidates who may already be earning millions of dollars. No candidate with any kind of business savvy would take up a position which entails greater responsibility for less reward.'

'Can you describe for us then how a CEO's salary is determined?'

'A CEO's salary, like any salary, is determined by the market. Which, in this case, would be the shareholders, represented by their elected board.'

'To be clear, "shareholders" refers to both individual investors, as well as institutions, like banks and mutual funds, and pension funds?'

'Indeed. Through those mechanisms, most citizens invest in the market in some form or another.'

'So professor, we could say that almost all working adults, and almost all retired folk, have already voted on this issue, and found CEOs worth every penny?'

'Yes, I think we can.'

'Thank you, professor.'

In Hugh's mind, the case might as well have concluded then and there. How could anyone argue against that? Even for Marshall, it was hopeless. Hugh had been skeptical of democracy in the past. Now, he believed in the will of the people more than he believed even in himself.

'Professor Colbert, you stated that it is possible to predict the success or transparency of a company based on the confidence and openness of the CEO,' Marshall began.

'Correct.'

'Couldn't it be the case that the CEO mirrors the state of the company?'

Hugh didn't like the way the professor adjusted his tie as he stared at Marshall.

'That the better a company performs, the more confident its CEO will feel – and act? And that more successful, more transparent companies will generally attract more successful, more transparent leaders?'

'Of course, we cannot rule that out-'

'Professor, what in your research would you say are the key traits of a successful CEO?'

'Organizations need different types of leadership at different times.'

'I see. So you'd agree that a company with a CEO who can change leadership style at the click of a button, so to speak, or even to switch CEOs as the situation demanded, with no expenses incurred, would have an advantage over one which must spend months, or years, along with millions of dollars, going through the firing and hiring and handover process?'

'Objection!' Joseph exclaimed, 'This is not supposed to be an exercise in hypotheticals!'

'Your honor, this is anything but a hypothetical situation. Rather, it is the exact situation we are gathered here to debate. Allow me to make my question more specific. All else being equal, professor, would you agree that the AutoCEO's ability to change leadership styles on an as-needed basis, or even to replace one persona with another, might represent a competitive advantage?'

'I suppose.'

'You mention that CEOs, and leadership generally, are of great importance. You are aware, I assume, of Professor Fennick's research, which shows CEOs are of especial importance when they are bad?'

Colbert cleared his throat. 'The research does suggest that a poorly performing or high risk-taking CEO will have a greater negative impact on a firm than the positive impact a high performing, more responsible CEO would have.'

'And this holds when examining specific duties associated with CEOs? For example, the CEO letter? Would you agree that a badly written letter from the CEO will have a worse impact on a company than no letter at all?'

'Yes, that is true.'

'Professor, you have also described the fact that most citizens are invested in the market in some form as a vote of approval for CEO pay.'

'That is correct.'

'Yet, isn't it true that research published by your own faculty also shows the majority of citizens oppose excessive CEO compensation? That they believe that current levels of pay are far too high?'

'That is correct. But it is also true that the vast majority of the public are poorly informed about how much CEOs are paid.'

Marshall paused to look at his papers dramatically. 'It says here that respondents consistently *under*-estimated how much CEOs earn by a wide margin. Isn't it reasonable to assume, then, that if the public were aware of how much CEOs actually earn, they would be even less supportive?'

'Objection! Again, we are not here to play hypotheticals!'

Marshall held up his hands. 'Professor, can you explain for us exactly how CEO's salaries reflect the market's decision-making then?'

'The market is often described as a voting machine – a system in which every share gives the people a voice.'

'Some investors own many shares, others, only a few?'

'True.'

'So those with the most shares – the wealthiest – can afford to shout the loudest?'

'In a manner of speaking.'

'Would you say that explains, professor, why, even though the majority of citizens disapprove of CEO compensation above $1 million per year, the shareholders who control the most votes, who are themselves the wealthiest, consistently vote to approve these packages?'

The professor frowned. 'A large number of shares are actually owned by citizens in mutual funds and managed funds. The pensions of firefighters and garbage collectors and teachers. Voted in blocks by their managers.'

'And do these fund managers consult the thousands or tens of thousands of citizens they are voting on behalf of? Do they ensure each member is aware of the issues, and canvass their opinions?'

'Not typically.'

'How often would you say that sort of consultation occurs?'

'I can't say I've heard of it.'

'How can you possibly use these votes as evidence of citizen's approval then? If they aren't even informed or consulted?' Marshall shook his head. 'In spite of this lack of consultation,' he continued, 'isn't it true that some fund managers have come under pressure in recent years from members' advocates to vote down compensation packages they consider excessive?'

'Yes.'

'And how many of those compensation packages would you estimate are passed anyway?

'The majority. But it's important to note that some institutional investors have indeed listened to members and voted nay.'

'How does that happen? If individual citizens disapprove of current levels of CEO pay, and even institutional investors are beginning to vote against large compensation packages?'

'The votes are often non-binding. The board members, who are ultimately tasked with the prudent running of the company, have the final say.'

'Ah yes,' Marshall rocked back on his heels. 'The boards who are often handpicked by the CEO. Who experience very little turnover, and run largely unopposed in elections. What percentage of board members did you find won re-election?'

The professor coughed. 'More than 99%. Which, I believe, demonstrates an extraordinary amount of confidence in the composition of these boards.'

'Or an extraordinary lack of choice. Or an extraordinary sense of apathy.' Marshall paced the room. Hugh heard every footstep land on the carpet. 'Professor Colbert, my learned colleague asked you how a board can know when a CEO is being paid too much. I would like you to name a figure. Is it a hundred times? A thousand times higher than their average worker's pay?'

'Without the right strategy, a CEO can destroy all the jobs underneath them. So it's meaningless to debate whether a CEO should earn a hundred, two hundred, or even a thousand times the typical worker, because there is no objective standard. It's completely arbitrary.'

'Completely arbitrary,' Marshall repeated. 'I'm not sure a worker struggling to get by would see it that way. To put that into perspective, ladies and gentlemen, a 200:1 ratio means that by lunchtime on January first, a CEO earning 200 times what their typical employee does will have already earned as much as their typical employee will earn for the entire rest of the year. Are you suggesting this is a correct ratio, professor? On the basis that they have the power to destroy the jobs beneath them? I beg your pardon, but that sounds more like ransom than leadership.'

'There's no objective way to determine a "correct" ratio.' The professor waggled his fingers in derisive air-quotes. 'CEO compensation is subjective. It's based on human emotions. And my research suggests that criticisms of the earnings of the top CEOs are also motivated by human emotion: namely envy.'

'Are you suggesting it is merely "envy" that motivated those who campaigned against Mr. Jefferson when he won 'Most overpaid CEO of the year' after the company achieved record profits by raising the price of the life-saving drug Pyradine by 5,000%?'

'Yes. The evidence lies in the data from employee's approval of their CEO's salary. Those who have climbed the corporate ladder are more likely to approve of the salary the person at the top is receiving. Those making more than six figures are 82% more likely to approve of their CEO's salary. But even at the lower end of the scale – those making less than $25,000 a year – 72% of them approve of their CEO's salary.'

'How many of those making less than $25,000 a year know what their CEO is being paid?'

'I'm afraid I don't recall,' Colbert smiled.

'Let me refresh your memory, professor,' Marshall said, holding up a copy of his paper. 'I believe the figure was only a third. In fact,' Marshall held up another paper, 'more than half of all employees don't know how much the CEO of their company is paid.'

'That's hardly surprising, given that less than 1% of the 30 million companies in this country are publicly traded.'

'Isn't it also true that the general public consistently underestimates – by a considerable amount – how much CEOs earn?'

'That would depend on how you define "considerable",'

'Would you mind reading the highlighted passage?'

The professor took the paper. 'Most citizens believe that CEOs earn about $1 million a year.'

'A tiny fraction of what those gathered here today have reported in income,' Marshall summarized. 'The actual disclosed pay at the top 500 companies in this country is more than ten times what the average citizen believes they earn. Professor, please tell us how much those who earned the least thought CEOs earned.'

Colbert cleared his throat and, reluctantly, began reading again. 'Those whose income was below $20,000 a year estimated CEO income at just $500,000 a year.'

'That's less than what Mr. Richardson here earns every week. If most of those respondents disapproved of CEOs like Mr. Richardson earning $500,000 each year, imagine how many would disapprove of him earning that figure every week. Even those in higher income brackets underestimated CEOs' pay, believing it to average around $5 million a year. Mr. Richardson makes more than that in a month. We may live in a divided nation in many respects, but if there is one thing people across the political aisle are united on, it is that CEOs make far too much, with 74% agreeing that CEOs are "vastly overpaid", and 62% suggesting there should be a cap. Wouldn't it be fair to conclude that if people knew how much CEOs are really paid, the figure who disapprove would be even higher?'

The professor smiled. 'I think it's fair to conclude that the average joe is indeed ignorant when it comes to CEO pay. So there's little reason to believe their estimations of how deserving CEOs are of that pay would be any less poorly informed. If the experts cannot agree on a single best method to measure CEO performance, why should we expect ill-informed citizens with no data at their disposal to do a better job?'

'I'm glad you bring up information, professor. Isn't it more accurate to say that this is not merely a case of ignorance, but one of misinformation? Misinformation spread, inadvertently or otherwise, by the media, which is itself owned by large corporations. And by politicians, who often come from big corporations, or are sponsored by them. In fact, in the last election one of the candidates drew attention to the fact that the CEOs of large firms earned more than 200 times the average worker. Professor, what was the real figure at the time?'

'Closer to four hundred.'

'Your own position, and by extension, your research, is also funded by two large corporations, is it not?'

'The department has been fortunate to enjoy the support of PharmaX and Hardings' for years. But the suggestion that this has led to any sort of bias in research is completely unfounded!'

'I see. It's merely a coincidence that you happen to be testifying on behalf of a class which includes the former CEOs of these two corporations? The very CEOs who sponsored your chair? And that several of the CEOs represented in this case have been the subjects of specific questionnaires about whether CEOs are overpaid? Fifty-nine percent of respondents believed Mr. Park is overpaid. Sixty-seven percent think Ms. Frost is overpaid. Sixty-eight believe Mr. Harding is overpaid. Seventy percent consider Mr. Jefferson overpaid.'

The professor waved his hands. 'Those figures are nothing more than a popularity contest. What a surprise! More people think the CEOs of a bank and a pharmaceutical company are overpaid than the CEOs of their favorite tech and toy companies.'

'I won't deny that popularity may have biased respondents somewhat. But the findings are clear. The vast majority of the general public believe CEOs and other top executives make too much money. Few thought they were paid the correct amount, and only a tiny, tiny, sliver thought any CEO was paid too little.'

The professor frowned. 'Perhaps. But even if you believe a CEO is overpaid by a million dollars, or ten million dollars, in the greater context of a large company, say the size of PearShape or PharmaX, this amounts to no more than a rounding error.'

'A rounding error! It's funny you mention that, professor. Last year, PharmaX sought to recoup wages from workers when it was revealed that they had been overpaid by 2c an hour for a single week. And yet, you describe ten million as a rounding error?'

'If a CEO can increase the value of a $100 billion company by 1%, that's equivalent to producing a billion dollars in value. It makes sense for big companies to pay big bucks, so to speak. For CEOs to share in the enormous value they're creating.'

'What about the CEO who decreases a company's value by 1%? That equates to a rather enormous loss'

'A CEO cannot be held solely responsible for such large losses.'

'How can they be given credit for such massive gains, then? And what evidence do you have that a CEO can impact a company this much – either positively or negatively?'

'Perhaps the most famous example of a CEO impacting a company is that of Dan Wang. His company faltered once he left, and only regained its footing once he returned.'

'What was the salary he returned for?'

'I'm not sure how that's relevant.'

'A token salary of $1 a year, if I'm not mistaken. If, indeed, Mr. Wang's reason was the main reason for the company's renewal – as a result of his fresh ideas, rather than just his symbolic installation – doesn't that demonstrate performance is not tied to salary?'

'Mr. Wang received a large compensation through other means.'

'That's true,' Marshall conceded. 'Of course, we would be remiss not to mention Mr. Wang without acknowledging another famous $1-a-year CEO, Mr. Skum.'

The professor's chair creaked.

'Isn't it true that since Mr. Skum took over Shouter, the company has shed more than half of its employees – and half of its most lucrative customers?'

'A CEO must put in place strategies to achieve stakeholder objectives.'

'And who are those stakeholders?'

'Well, shareholders, of course,' Professor Colbert answered. 'And employees,' he added, like an afterthought. Hugh breathed a sigh of relief.

'And what would some of their objectives be?'

'Generally, shareholders want to see growth, both in profits and share price.'

'What about dividends? The actual earnings they receive from the company?'

The professor smiled. 'Dividends are no longer as important as they were in the past. As we see more institutional investors, and more trading, few people are holding onto their shares long enough to receive a dividend. The goal is to buy low and sell high.'

'Is that investing?'

'In a form. When the time between buying and selling is particularly short, it might be better characterized as trading.'

'And what about the employees? What are their objectives?'

'A rewarding work environment, with some security, and the ability to grow in their careers.'

'"Some" security, you say?'

'Well, total security is not possible.'

'I'm sorry,' Marshall spent a moment fumbling through his papers.

'Did you not say you were a *tenured* professor?'

Colbert grunted. 'Workers need to recognize that instead of long careers spent at a single company, as their fathers or grandfathers might have experienced, today's employee must be flexible. Ready to pick up new skills and work in new places. The average employee will change jobs three to seven times over the course of their working life. That's a new job every seven years or so.'

'Approximately the average tenure of a CEO.'

'Indeed. In fact, some studies show that young people are changing jobs even more often. While the previous generation averaged about two jobs in their first decade post college, it's now double. A job change, or even an entire career change, every two to three years. That's the reality of today's job market.'

'Professor Colbert, my question was about employees' objectives – not their realities. Isn't it true that every year, your surveys show that employees rank job security as one of the most important features of their work? Even above the amount they're paid?'

'Well, yes.'

'And have CEOs prioritized the job security of their employees as one of their key objectives?'

'The current market doesn't allow -'

'Yes or no, professor?'

'No.'

'Would you characterize the CEO's position as one with an inherent conflict of interest?'

'I'm afraid I don't understand the question.'

'Isn't it impossible for any CEO to prioritize the needs and wants of their employees, their shareholders, and other stakeholders all at once?'

'Certainly, the CEO's role is a complex one.'

'Where a CEO is forced to decide between prioritizing the desires of employees for, say, a break room, or an increase to their hourly pay, which will typically be prioritized?'

'Legally speaking, the company has a responsibility to maximize profits for the shareholder. So long as a worker's basic rights are respected – such as them being given their legally mandated break, or paid the minimum wage – the company has fulfilled its obligations.'

'So the CEO does not, in fact, prioritize employees' objectives.'

'Unless it can be demonstrated that a break room or a wage increase would lead to improvement in productivity. And in turn, a lift in profits.'

'And this would need to be demonstrated in advance?' Marshall asked. 'The company would not raise workers' wages and measure the degree to which performance improved?'

Colbert laughed. 'That would be absurd!'

'Funny,' Marshall said, turning on his heel. 'Isn't that how CEOs are motivated? Pay first, measure later?'

'A CEO's role is complex and multifaceted. But in a well-run company, the goals of investors and employees are in harmony. What is best for employees tends to be what is best for the company. And what is best for the company tends to be best for the shareholders.'

'Fascinating. Can you think of any examples where that might not hold true?'

Colbert gulped. 'Not really.'

'What about offshoring? Would sending workers' jobs overseas be good for the employees?'

'Well, not for those specific employees. But we need to take a global view here. Offshoring provides incredible opportunities for people in other countries. People who might not have had access to work otherwise.'

'Opportunities which have been described, and I am quoting from your own university's human rights research committee, as "modern-day slavery". Again, and I quote, more than forty million people are in slavery today. Over a quarter of whom are children. The offshore subsidiaries of both Mr. Park and Ms. Frost's companies were mentioned by name. Along with reports of grueling 18-hour days, appalling living conditions, only one day off a year, and an extremely high number of workplace accidents. Including the case of a teenage girl who was blinded while producing dolls for ToyStar. Would you describe those opportunities as beneficial?'

'Not all offshore operations are like that.'

'What about automation, professor? Would you describe automation as beneficial to employees?'

The professor looked to be on firmer footing here. He nodded enthusiastically.

'Automation has improved the lives of many employees. Helping them avoid repetitive actions associated with injuries. Assisting them to perform better in their jobs. You could say automation is one of those win-wins. Both employees and investors benefit.'

'How do investors benefit?'

'Through higher efficiency and lower costs'. The professor looked at Marshall as if he were the dunce of the class.

'Lower costs?' Marshall played up the dunce act, even pausing to scratch his head. 'I would have thought all those machines would be expensive. Not to mention the software development costs.'

Colbert cleared his throat. 'There is usually a certain amount of… downsizing associated with automation.'

'Mass layoffs, in other words. Would you describe losing your job as beneficial to employees? After all, isn't that what we're here to discuss today? The damage caused by losing one's job?' Marshall gestured towards Hugh and the others. 'I'll ask you again Professor. Is losing your job generally perceived as beneficial?'

'I suppose not. But this is one example of the tough decisions a CEO has to make sometimes.'

'To automate a job which can be done more cost effectively, or more accurately and safely, by a machine?'

'Yes. You have to understand the CEO's position here. To not automate would violate the company's primary responsibility of creating shareholder value. Especially if other firms are making these efficiencies.'

'I see. And couldn't the same be said, then, of the CEO's position?'

'I- I-'

'No further questions.'

CHAPTER 17

Hugh rubbed his sleep-filled eyes. Blinked.

There he was. That little weasel, Jai, was on the stand.

In all the lawsuits Hugh had ever been involved in as a defendant, his counsel had been unequivocal in its advice: don't take the stand. You'll just look guilty.

Those had been Marshall's exact words. And yet, here Marshall was, questioning Jai. As if he had more faith in the weaselly programmer than he did in Hugh.

'Mr. Kapoor. Could you explain how the AutoAutomator software performs its task of optimizing business? With specific regard to the decision to automate or outsource positions?'

Breakfast – eggs, Cheltenham bacon, and liqueur coffee – gurgled around Hugh's stomach. Although they were more than halfway through the trial, he still wasn't used to the 9AM starts.

Jai looked more nervous than pleased. Hugh would have thought he'd be jumping at the chance to explain the benefits of his nasty piece of software.

'The AutoAutomator uses big data to calculate the difference between what an employee is currently being paid, and how much it would cost for their role to be automated or outsourced. Then, it undertakes a cost-benefit analysis, to determine what non-financial benefits and drawbacks automation or outsourcing might have.'

'But Mr. Kapoor,' Marshall put on a puzzled face, 'We have heard that it is impossible to determine a correct ratio for CEO to worker pay. How can your software undertake such cost-benefit analyses on an even larger scale?'

Jai pushed up his glasses. 'Simply because something is something is difficult to determine does not mean a range cannot be calculated. That's what Ms. Dryser was hired by Mr. Richardson to do.'

'Objection! Speculation.'

'Sustained. Please refrain from inferring the reasons for the complainant's behavior, or the methods employed by Ms. Dryser.'

'I'll reframe my question; how does AutoAutomator calculate ranges?'

'There are many measurements for which calculating a precise figure is impossible. Take body temperature. A healthy body temperature can vary depending on age, ethnicity, and level of activity.'

'Objection! Relevance!' Having hit once, Joseph looked keen to strike again.

'Overruled. You may continue, Mr. Kapoor.'

'Rather than saying, "nobody can say what the ideal body temperature is," the medical profession has determined a range of normal temperatures based upon thousands of participants in diverse medical trials. The same is true of blood sugar. Or heart rates. In the same way, the AutoAutomator determines a range of CEO compensation, based on the data of thousands of companies.'

'And what did your data show? Can you give us a summary?'

'The software confirmed that the more CEOs get paid, the worse their companies perform over the next three years. This is nothing new – academic studies found much the same thing years ago.'

'Fascinating. Mr. Kapoor, we've heard predictions that CEOs will make the best decisions for a company when they have "skin in the game". Can you explain what that means?'

'If a CEO is exposed to some risk by having some of their assets tied to the company's performance, they're assumed to have an incentive to perform better.'

'Like ownership of company stock?'

'Exactly. That's part of the justification for large chunks of a CEO's pay coming in the form of stocks and options. Aside, of course, from the tax benefits to the company.'

'And does the evidence support this theory?'

'Past studies struggled to find a relationship between CEO pay or investment and company performance. But our analysis of 1,500 companies over the past two decades showed that the more CEOs are paid – through any means – the worse their companies do. And that's after accounting for external variables, like general market conditions or a particular industry's outlook.'

Hugh's stomach grumbled again. He wished he hadn't had a second helping of that bacon. Or at least, he wished he'd trimmed the fat just a little.

'The software focused on how a company performed relative to other companies in its field at the time. And the worst effects on performance were observed in those companies where CEOs were paid the most. While there were exceptions, generally speaking, companies who paid their CEOs amounts in the top 10% had the worst performance. They return 10% less to their shareholders than their industry peers. Looking at the very top – the 5% highest-paid CEOs – the results are even worse. Their companies performed on average 15% worse than their peers.'

'What causes this?'

'Of course, there's only so far the analysis can take us,' Jai conceded. 'We're only looking at numbers here. But past research – which has also been fed into the database – suggests it's linked to confidence. Overconfidence, specifically. CEOs paid huge amounts of money tend to think less critically about their decisions. They ignore data which doesn't confirm what they've already been convinced of, which results in over-investing.'

'What is "over-investing"?'

'When a company invests too much, and in the wrong sorts of products. Ones which don't yield positive returns for investors.'

'And what are the consequences of poor or negative yields for CEOs?'

'Often, there are none.'

'What sorts of circumstances lead to CEOs losing their jobs then?'

When your damn software automates them away, Hugh felt like shouting. He swallowed, willing his anger – along with the eggs and bacon – to settle down.

'Sometimes, a CEO is made redundant – such as when a company merges with another, and only one is required. Sometimes, it's a regular transition. Where the CEO is retiring, taking up a better position, or has stepped down because of health or stress-related reasons. Or, as our data has shown, as CEOs are aging, many have died whilst in office.'

'Now, that's a risk we wouldn't associate with the AutoCEO!' Marshall beamed.

'Indeed. Finally, there are some performance-related transitions. Where the CEO was asked to leave by the board of directors.'

'And what about personal reasons?' Marshall was putting on his fake puzzled face again.

'There are of course a large number of transitions that are recorded as due to "personal reasons". But analysis revealed these departures are almost always correlated with poor financial performance.'

'So the software would classify those as performance-related?'

'Yes. It may be that a CEO's personal problems are causing them to exhibit leadership problems. Or, it may be that a company's financial woes add to the CEO's personal woes, which in turn results in their departure under the guise of 'personal reasons', adding to the company's instability. Either way, the AutoCEO removes this personal element.'

'Does your research show any changes to CEO departures over the years?'

'The turnover rate has increased. Rather than spending almost a decade in their positions, CEOs now leave after about seven years.'

'The seven-year itch?' Marshall smiled.

'It would appear so, with a 130% increase in performance-related transitions. Even though CEOs here still have some of the longest average tenures in the world, with their international counterparts much more likely to be dismissed for poor performance, boards are increasingly asking their CEOs to leave because the company is doing poorly.'

'What sorts of reasons are there for "performance-related" decisions?'

'When a bubble bursts, the software found large numbers of CEOs in that industry being thrown under the bus. In the wake of the telecommunications and IT industry collapses, the average tenure of CEOs in those fields halved. Even though they may well have been managing the industry-wide downturn as best they could.'

'Does your analysis reveal any rationale behind this?'

'It would seem that today, shareholders – particularly the big, powerful voting blocks – assess every company against every other company, rather than considering whether a particular company is performing well relative to others in its industry.'

See? Hugh wanted to shout. It's not our fault! It's the people!

He bit his tongue, sweet blood mingling with the aftertaste of eggs in his saliva.

'What effect does that have on the markets?'

'Professional investors rush from one industry to another. They dump stocks that have anything to do with an under-performing industry, rather than investing for the long-term. As a result, boards try to keep their companies competitive by firing CEOs whenever the industry experiences a bump.'

'Isn't that a good thing for shareholders?'

'Were it not for the golden parachutes many of these CEOs get. With very few ways to claw money back from under-performing CEOs, and with the extravagant packages most are guaranteed upon leaving, not to mention the costs involved in hiring a new CEO, the whole process can end up costing a company tens of millions. At a time when it's already performing badly.'

'Claw back? Can you explain that term, please?'

'Deductions for negative performance. Our analysis shows that a

CEO is generally rewarded whenever the company does well. But has no money or perks taken away when the company slips in its rankings, profit, or other measures.'

'Is there any evidence to show that clawing money back might work?'

'Evidence is scant, because these provisions are almost never made in CEO's contracts. In fact, that's one of the key shareholder complaints uncovered in the AutoAutomator's analysis. Yet, most CEOs endorse these sorts of provisions in the contracts of the staff who work beneath them. Workers at the factories that produce Ms. Frost's dolls, for instance, are penalized 30 minutes' salary for five minutes' tardiness. They're docked pay for losing their ID cards. Using too much toilet paper. Even forced to forfeit two-and-a-half months' salary if they decide to quit.'

'Objection! Those are the rules of the companies ToyStar outsources to, not Ms. Frost's policies!'

'Overruled.'

Jai shrugged. 'Even onshore, workers are docked pay for showing up to work late. Spending too long in the bathroom. Or wasting office supplies. Yet when a CEO's negligence, or personal scandals, cause a company's stock price to tank, resulting in a loss of income for workers and investors, there is no provision to get back some of the millions they've been awarded for sinking the ship.'

'Has your analysis uncovered other ways CEO pay can be better managed?'

'One possibility is indexing compensation to relative performance. This would ensure, for example, that the CEO of an oil company is paid for improvements his leadership made to the company. Not because oil prices generally went up. Under such a model, bonuses and performance-based pay would be calculated relative to the company's performance relative to other companies. Not just based on whether its stock went up or down. But this sort of policy is also rare.'

'Did your software find this kind of method of calculation in the contracts of any of the gentlemen – or lady – here?'

'No. In fact, terminating the employment of a CEO – with a generous separation package – was the most frequently used method by far.'

'You're saying that so-called "performance-related" firings often fail to improve company performance?'

'That's often the case. Other times, an actual decline in the CEO's performance is noted. And often, CEOs fired for a decline in their performance actually started out by outperforming their peers.'

'So the system rewards mediocrity?'

'Exactly. In as much as CEOs can or do affect a company's fate, it's better for the CEO if the company performs "okay" all the time, rather than for it to do very well, and then drop to "okay", or worse'.

'Based on the AutoAutomator's analysis, does changing CEO help?'

'Good performance of a company does appear correlated with the longevity of its CEO. But as for whether good performance leads to longevity, or longevity leads to good performance, the data is inconclusive.'

'I see. Mr. Kapoor, several expert witnesses have testified to the intelligence – or otherwise – of CEOs. What factors has your software identified?'

'Well, CEOs are 0.5 standard deviations above average in height. In fact, AutoAutomator's analysis shows that people in the bottom quartile have almost no chance of becoming the CEO of a large corporation.'

'Does the data show any particular advantage to height? Intelligence, decision-making ability, strategizing, teamwork? Or any of the other qualities we have heard about?'

'No. Height has very little to do with any of those attributes.'

Hugh scoffed. Of course a shortass like Jai would say that.

'However, height does appear correlated with confidence.'

Another tick in Hugh's box!

'Psychology suggests this may be related to dominance, is that correct?'

'Yes. Linguistic analysis shows people describe others as looking down upon those they consider – metaphorically, or in this case, also literally – beneath them. Or looking up to leaders. Discrimination based on height is largely unconscious, but may contribute to some of the bias experienced by people of typically slighter statures'

'What evidence do you have to back this up?'

'More than intelligence, and more than height, measures of psychological fitness for the military are a good predictor of likelihood of becoming a CEO. Some analysts claim that CEOs use dominance rather than intelligence to convince others.'

'So for all the talk of intelligence and team work we've heard, the physical and mental ability to command others, to look and feel confident in oneself, is more important?'

Hugh glowered at Jai, willing him to shut up.

'It would appear that way. Extroversion and contentiousness also showed up as more important than intelligence. Psychological evidence indicates we perceive CEOs as more intelligent than they are, simply because they are rich and powerful. We believe they must have been intelligent to amass all that wealth and power. In short, they're thought to be smart because they look smart. Looks might fool people, but they don't fool the algorithm.'

Again, Hugh thought, Jai would say that. His looks weren't fooling anyone.

'Speaking of looks, does your research indicate which is more important to people's perceptions – looks or intelligence?'

'According to the AutoAutomator's analysis, we – by which I mean the general public, along with a company's employees, shareholders, and even board – look for both in a CEO. Looks and smarts. We want our CEOs to look the part and be able to make intelligent decisions. And while there may be some CEOs who have both, they are few and far between. But it appears that many CEOs possess neither attribute. Our algorithms find that CEOs are neither of above average intelligence, nor of above average looks, as rated by human peers.'

Hugh bristled. Sure, he didn't look great in gym shorts. Sure, he preferred candlelit restaurants - but that was a mark of sophistication. Besides, he had a good side. How dare Jai say he was not of above average looks!

'It's more a look of "competence" than conventional attractiveness,' Jai continued. 'And even this is factored into CEO pay. Take them out of their tailored suits, and they look the same as any other middle-aged white male.'

He knew he should have worn one of his best suits today, rather than this ill-fitting bargain-basement trash Joseph had recommended.

'So they might look like a factory machinist, say? Or a union worker?'

A union worker! Now that was taking things too far.

'As long as they don't open their mouths!' Jai laughed. 'Shiny white teeth are a dead giveaway – CEOs can afford much better dentistry.'

Hugh ran his tongue across the veneers CGM had paid for. They were, after all, a business expense. Jai was practically confirming that.

'In fact,' Jai continued, 'perhaps the single most damning piece of evidence which shows that CEOs do not get where they are based on talent alone is the fact that the C-suite is so dominated by white men. Let me rephrase that. To say white men dominate the Fobbs 500 list is an understatement. Fewer than 2% of CEOs are non-white. And of all the companies, just one is led by an openly gay CEO. Not only are white males the majority by a longshot, but they are by far the best compensated group.'

'How would the Fobbs 500 look if the leadership were more representative of broader society?'

'Across all 500 companies, there are only 22 women at the top – most of whom were hired only recently. That's more than ten times fewer than the 250 women who should be there if all things were equal. Only 8% of the top earners are women, and even at this level, there is a pay gap of 18%.'

'What does the software say about that pay gap? Is it explained by less experience?'

Jai shook his head. 'Not at all. Most of the women who make it to CEO are smarter than their male peers. They tend to have more, higher degrees, from better respected institutions. And female CEOs tend to have better approval ratings than their male counterparts, too. Yet the best-paid male CEO last year received a salary 1726% higher than that of the best-paid female CEO. A lack of female leadership at the very top is symptomatic of a lack of female leadership at other levels, too. Not a single one of the top companies has more than three women in executive positions. But studies have shown that you need at least three women in leadership to achieve a critical mass and see a change in corporate culture.'

'So CEOs are paid millions of dollars not to shape corporate culture but to have shiny white teeth and look the part. A part which includes being white and male?'

'It sounds ludicrous and circular – but that's because it is. We expect CEOs to look a certain way, which includes splashing money about in a certain way. And hence, we pay them a certain amount to keep up that lifestyle. Private jets, flashy watches, boozy parties, and of course, bright white teeth. More than businesspeople or entrepreneurs, our analysis shows that CEOs share more traits with royalty, or even, concepts of gods.'

Now, there was another quote Hugh would pay to see immortalized on the back of his book: that he had more in common with royalty, or a god.

'Gods?'

'In a certain sense. Not the omnipotent creator figures you might think of when you hear the word. But the kind that appear in parables – ones that, if people stop believing in them, lose their power.'

'Have CEOs lost their power? Does the data indicate whether people have ceased to believe in them?'

'Not entirely. Not yet. But the public has been losing faith for a long time. My prediction is that more people will cease to revere CEOs as AutoCEOs become more common.'

Hugh stared. Was this really Jai? He sounded drunk on power.

'Why is that?'

'Because anything a human CEO can do, an AutoCEO can do better. An AutoCEO like Mike J. Guy not only draws on the intelligence – and emotional intelligence – of the best past and present CEOs, while learning from the mistakes of the worst. It also has a secret weapon.'

'What's that?' Marshall leaned in, as if Jai were about to tell him a delicious secret.

'Without spending a cent, an AutoCEO can have brighter teeth than anyone else on the planet. It's just a matter of manipulating the white balance.'

Hugh closed his mouth, suddenly concerned he might have Cheltenham bacon stuck in his teeth.

Joseph stood. 'Mr. Kapoor, you claim that the more CEOs get paid, the worse their companies perform. Isn't it possible that another explanation for their performance in the market might be a result of what Professor Colbert has suggested? That shareholders react negatively - that is, with envy – to high CEO pay?'

'Actually,' Jai coughed, 'both stock performance and accounting performance suffer. The company drops in real performance as well.'

Hugh felt hot. It must be this awful polyester blend suit.

'You described overpaid CEOs as "overinvesting" in products that don't yield positive returns for investors. What evidence do you have?'

'Looking at the 150 CEOs paid the least, 13% completed mergers over the past year, making their companies a negative 0.5% return.'

'See!' Hugh interjected. 'You need to pay CEOs more if you want a good return!' Joseph's angry glare was even worse than the judge's reprimand.

'Mr. Kapoor, please continue with your analysis.'

'Of the best-paid CEOs, 19% did mergers. And those deals resulted in a negative 1.4% return over the following three years. In other words, the worst-paid CEOs actually performed better – even though they too made a loss.'

Joseph frowned. 'But that's over a three-year period. Perhaps their decisions pan-out over the long-term?'

'Maybe. But most CEOs and board members have a short-term focus. Like governments, they're concerned about reelection. So it is reasonable to assume they would look to make investments which would deliver positive results in the short-term. And our analysis points to this too.' Jai shuffled some papers on his desk.

Gloating, Hugh folded his arms in front of his chest. Jai didn't look so smart now, without his screens and his multi-buttoned mouse.

'The longer a CEO's tenure, the more pronounced the firm's poor performance. The longer a CEO retains that position, the more able they are to appoint allies to their board who are willing to go along with bad decisions. CEOs who exhibit high overconfidence over a long tenure return 22% worse shareholder value compared to their peers. And it's not just shareholders who suffer from their poor performance. Our data shows that CEOs aren't great at timing the market for themselves either. Of the firms which paid their CEOs the least, a third held into their options when they could have cashed them in for a profit.'

Hugh bit his tongue, and let Joseph do the work for him.

'Surely that demonstrates that highly-paid CEOs are paid more because they make better investment decisions.'

'On the contrary. More than twice as many high-paid CEOs – almost 90%, in fact – made the same mistake.'

Hugh could almost see Joseph backpedaling.

'Mr. Kapoor, you also indicated that boards are asking CEOs to leave when a company is performing poorly, correct?'

'That's right.'

'Doesn't this indicate that boards recognize the CEO is indeed the most important factor in a company's success?'

'According to the AutoAutomator's output, it appears that the CEO is often a useful scapegoat in these situations. But the main increase in CEO departures remains as a result of mergers.'

'But Mr. Kapoor, don't mergers provide an opportunity to examine CEO performance? For the board to select the best candidate from the two original companies to run the merger?'

'Again, the existing research, and the data from the AutoAutomator, doesn't back that up. The mechanisms and logic of mergers have been widely studied. But it's generally agreed that the final selection of the CEO has very little to do with the individual's performance.'

'Assuming for the moment that your data regarding CEO selection is accurate,'

'It is,' Jai insisted.

'How do you account for the fact that the complainants have also been replaced as board members? Doesn't that demonstrate overreach? That the software has gone too far?'

'The service AutoAutomator was contracted to supply extends to all positions in the company's employ. When the software found that each of these former CEOs' positions could be more profitably and beneficially carried out by an AutoCEO, that judgment reflected on each of them not only as CEOs, but as board members.'

'How do you possibly justify that?'

'One of the most influential factors in the algorithm's weighting was the fact that by sitting on one another's boards, each member's ability to be fair and impartial was compromised. As shown in decisions about CEO compensation. Moreover, if the board is tasked with finding and retaining appropriate talent, and the CEO is found to have not performed adequately, then by definition, the board has failed.

Either by misidentifying talent in the first place, or by inappropriately incentivizing the CEO since. According to the software, not only were the complainants assessed as inadequate in their role as CEOs. But by endorsing one anothers' lackluster performance, they demonstrated inadequacy as board members, too.'

'How convenient. Is that all your software's analysis has to go on?'

Jai shook his head. 'The AutoAutomator additionally calculated that, as members of each others' boards, these former CEOs were paid $100,000 to $200,000 a year. Plus perks. For a job that requires, at most, 200 to 300 hours of work. That's the equivalent of an hourly rate of $300 to $1000 – for duties which the AutoBoard can perform for pennies.'

Hugh almost spat his water across the desk. AutoBoard! This was the first he'd heard of any AutoBoard!

'AutoBoard? Are you suggesting a piece of software can replace not only an individual CEO, but the expertise, oversight, and feedback of an entire board of CEOs?'

Somehow, Joseph managed to make his eyes pop, as if Jai's claim were the most dazzlingly outrageous thing he'd ever heard.

'Our analysis showed there is very little evidence to suggest boards, at least in their human form, actually aid company performance. Boards are meant to function as independent oversight groups. To act in the best interest of the company's shareholders, as you mention. But what we find, when boards are stacked with fellow CEOs, is that they are actually in league with the CEO. They don't have enough distance from the CEO. The CEO is often a personal friend, as is the case, for example, with Mr. Richardson and Mr. Harding, or even, a family member. Some CEOs even chair their own boards! It is impossible for such a board to provide unbiased feedback.'

'What evidence do you have to back up this statement?'

'The AutoAutomator drew on data from a study of over 26,000 board appointments over a five-year period. It found that 1,731 board members were also CEOs.'

'That's a small proportion.'

'True. But this group of CEOs – of which the complainants are members – have deeply interwoven relationships. Company A has a board member from Company B, and Company B has a board member from Company A.'

'Surely that's a relatively rare occurrence.'

'There are others who try to paper a veneer of respectability over the whole arrangement. But the AutoAutomator still found them out. To appear less biased and insular, Company A might have a board member from Company B. In turn, B has one from C, who has a member from Company A. In most cases, CEOs end up sitting on the boards of other large companies, who have similar structures to their own firms. This is not a case of established CEOs mentoring newcomers. Nor of young blood being brought in with fresh ideas. Rather, it's the same old established guard. Recirculating their same old established ideas. Patting each other on the back.'

Hugh sighed with relief. At least Jai had described what they did as a 'pat on the back.' He'd heard worse analogies.

'The AutoAutomator found no significant influence on the part of these CEO board members. Either in terms of improved oversight, or executive compensation. The only exception was when CEOs sat on each other's boards.'

'So you admit that hiring experienced, professional CEOs as board members can indeed have a positive impact on companies in the types of reciprocal arrangements my clients engaged in.'

'On the contrary. The impact in such cases was wholly negative. Hiring CEOs to the board generally results in no impact at all. Or, where there are incestuous relationships between companies, negative ones. First and foremost is the issue of CEO compensation. It's in a CEO's interests to boost the compensation of a fellow CEO, increasing the average so they will enjoy a higher rate of pay the next time their own compensation is due for review. But it goes much further than that. There are conflicts of interest to consider, for instance, or even corporate espionage.'

'Mr. Kapoor, those are very serious allegations. I would caution you not to make unsubstantiated claims.'

Jai waved a hand, casual once more. Hugh couldn't believe the transformation he'd undergone. From quiet mouse in the office, quivering wreck taking the stand, to now, this cavalier attitude. Arm him with data, and Jai thought the world belonged to him.

'This is all a matter of public record. The CEO of Myriad, for instance, was a member of the PearShape board for years. The two companies claim not to be in competition, but both make mobile phones, laptops, sell apps. Both developed their own internet browsers. Yet conflicts of interest occur even when companies aren't directly competing. They don't even have to be in the same industry.'

Joseph gave Jai a withering look. 'Surely that's taking it too far!'

'Mr. Harding and Mr. Richardson, for example, are the CEOs of a bank and a diversified company which primarily invests in telecommunications.'

Hugh looked around for a pen with which to jot that down.

'Not only are they the chairs of their own boards, but Mr. Richardson and Mr. Harding are members of each other's boards. A few years back, Mr. Harding appears to have been involved in some sort of a feud with his co-CEO at the time, Mr. Wiener. He needed the board's support to overthrow him. In order to secure Mr. Richardson's support, Mr. Harding asked one of his analysts to take a "fresh look" at the neutral rating he'd given CGM stock. The analyst, in turn, was trying to get his kids into St. Lucre's Preschool... so he asked Mr. Harding to pull some strings in exchange for taking this "fresh look". The bank donated a million dollars to St. Lucre's, the analyst's kids were enrolled, and voila, he upgraded CGM's rating from "neutral" to "buy". In turn, Mr. Richardson voted to oust Mr. Wiener.'

Hugh felt the heat blaze across his face. How dare Jai suggest he'd only voted to get rid of Wiener because of the rating upgrade! Sure, the upgrade sweetened the deal. But he would have ousted Wiener anyway. Because he was Pete's friend. And because Wiener had said something snide about his favorite watch manufacturer.

'With all due respect, Mr. Kapoor, other than Mr. Wiener, for whom was this arrangement a problem?'

'The swathes of investors who were given misleading information by an investment bank authority they trusted.'

CHAPTER 18

'Ms. Owen, can you explain how you know Mr. Richardson?'

Owen. So that was that dreadful Lila woman's last name. Funny, Hugh had always imagined it would be some sort of double-barrelled monstrosity. Then again, who would marry her?

He chuckled. Lila Owen. An apt name. He was sure she'd be owen' money here and owen' money there. Hugh bit his lip to stop himself from laughing out loud, the metallic tang of his own blood filling his mouth.

Still, her name was far from the only surprise. Since she'd taken the stand, Hugh had learned that Lila has a degree in labor history. But the biggest surprise was that Marshall, the very lawyer who had helped Hugh get out of numerous sticky situations Lila was always trying to trap him in, had somehow gotten Lila to testify for him. For the company. And on the side of automation, no less. Wasn't she supposed to be for workers' rights?

Hugh had never felt so betrayed in his life.

Marshall must have paid her, he decided.

'Certainly,' Lila said. She was wearing a proper jacket – at least, what passed for a proper jacket coming from someone like Lila's closet. A better fitting one than the suits the protesters wore outside of CGM's meetings. Even her hair color looked toned down.

It wasn't fair, Hugh thought, sucking on his newly-whitened teeth and running a hand over his newly-plugged scalp. They should be seeing the *real* Lila, not this fake version. Then they'd know not to listen to anything she had to say.

'In a way,' Hugh heard her say, 'it's more damaging than feudalism!'

Clearly, he'd missed quite a bit of her testimony. What was she banging on about now? Feudalism? Hugh didn't know exactly what that meant, but it sounded like something he'd sourced an essay from Pete about.

Hugh looked over at Joseph, wondering when he was going to step up to the plate. This wasn't supposed to be a history lesson!

'In what way?' Marshall asked in his infuriating, pondering way.

'In feudal times, everybody of a low-born household knew they would never rise to the levels of the lords and ladies. Knew they would never become royalty. Now, we're told everyone is equal. When we don't all become CEOs, we blame ourselves. Even though it's almost as impossible.'

'Surely all it takes is tenacity,' Marshall said, 'Grit!'

Hugh liked the sound of that. He wondered if, once all this blew over, he could get Marshall to write a blurb for his book: 'All it takes is tenacity and grit'.

'CEOs are more like kings than presidents,' Lila continued. 'They're not really elected to their positions. They're appointed. There's a lot more to it than tenacity and grit. If that really were all it took, we shouldn't see such enormous imbalances in who actually becomes

CEOs. It's significantly easier for a white male over the age of 50 with an ivy league education and a bunch of rich and powerful friends and family members to become a CEO than it is for anyone else.'

'Ms. Owen, how would you characterize the chances of a young black female born into a poor family who can't afford a university education until later in life of becoming a CEO?'

'About as good as the odds of her becoming a princess.'

'Objection! Your honor, we are not here to discuss the likelihood of becoming a princess, or slaying a dragon-'

'I will rephrase: wouldn't you agree that when someone fails to become royalty, we blame the system. But when they fail to succeed in business, we blame the individual?'

'Precisely.'

'And what are the effects of these sorts of gaps, between the haves and the have-nots?'

'In addition to the poverty, ill health, and lowered life expectancy suffered by individuals, at the societal level, high levels of economic inequality are associated with much lower levels of innovation, and higher levels of crime and political instability.'

'And what about within companies?'

'Companies with unexplained pay gaps – that is, huge CEO-to-worker pay ratios without economic factors that explain them – see their performance drop by as much as half compared to those with lower unexplained ratios. In a fifth of companies, not only is the CEO overpaid, but the other staff are underpaid.'

'Is there any evidence of improvements in this regard? Of companies adjusting to a fairer model?'

'On the contrary, the top 1% of earners now capture 95% of all income gains. Over the last half-century, the ratio between CEOs and workers has increased by a factor of ten. But it isn't just the growth in CEO pay that's behind this. We have to look at the other half of the equation, too.'

'What's that?'

'The fact that there has been slowing, even stagnant, and in some cases, negative wage growth for middle- and lower-class work. Mr. Park here was once the most unequal employer in the country, earning almost two thousand times what his average employee did. Of course, that honor now belongs to Ms. Frost.' Lila shot her a stern look.

'At one of the companies Mr. Park formerly led, he insisted on rolling out a controversial plan all at once. Across all stores, because he insisted the company needed a "quick result". Well, it certainly got one. During the just over 12 months Mr. Park acted as CEO, he caused the stock price to drop to less than half of the value it was when he took over. When sales plummeted, he blamed the customers instead of his own model.'

'What was the outcome?'

'More than 20,000 workers lost their jobs.'

'So did I!' Kim shouted.

The judge banged his gavel. Hugh was glad someone else was getting into trouble for once.

'Mr. Park may have lost his job,' Lila conceded once the furor died down. 'But he still walked away with a hell of a lot of money. As did the guy after him. And the guy after that.'

'Let me play devil's advocate for a moment,' Marshall smiled. He already was, Hugh thought. Marshall sold his soul the minute he refused to help him.

'Wouldn't a CEO who had an idea that could turn the company around and save the jobs of the remaining staff be well worth their salary?'

'Their idea might be, sure. But what we consistently observe is companies hiring people, not buying ideas. Rather than having prospective CEOs tender ideas and paying them once they're proven, like they'd commission any other contractor, instead they pay first and ask questions later. That,' Lila's eyes bored straight into Hugh's 'is why the AutoCEO will do a better job.'

Hugh had always known Lila was two-faced, but this was a level of traitorousness even he hadn't anticipated.

'Ms. Owen,' Joseph began, once the recess was through, and Hugh's bladder was as empty as his hopes. 'Is it not true that CEOs here have some of the most highly scrutinized pay packets on the planet? Their compensation is calculated by consultants. Justified by talent scientists and professors. Voted on by specialist committees. Recommended by boards, and approved by shareholders!'

'CEOs are in a unique position compared to other employees. Not only are they able to select their own compensation consultants and talent scientists, and sponsor research chairs who will churn out papers in support of their exorbitant salaries, but they are able to handpick committee and board members. Who in turn, all work in concert to manipulate shareholders. Several of the former CEOs here were members of their own boards, even as chair, or engaged in reciprocal arrangements whereby they sat on each others' boards. A factory worker or a waiter or a nurse or a teacher or a firefighter, has next to no influence over the people hiring and firing them.'

'You say that CEOs are in a unique position, Ms. Owen. Isn't it true that part of that unique position involves acting as a role model? As a philanthropist? And most importantly, as an inspiration? CEOs might buy flashy suits and cars, shiny watches and rings, but when they buy these things, they are not only spurring others on to greatness, they are also stimulating the economy.'

Joseph was on fire today. Spurring others on to greatness? Hugh wanted that on his book cover, too.

'The trickle-down effect?'

'Precisely.'

'There is a trickle-down effect,' Lila conceded, 'But not in the way you might imagine. When you give a person who doesn't have much money a little more, what do they do? They spend it. Not necessarily because they are bad at managing money. But because there are things they need and want. Give someone on minimum wage an extra $50, and they can afford a meal out. To take their kids to the pool, or the movies. To save up for a short holiday. Give it to someone earning millions – what is $50 to them? It will sit in their bank account unnoticed, unspent. Earning them even more money, rather than going back into the economy.'

'With all due respect, Ms. Owen, you've told us a great deal about what the trickle-down effect isn't. What do you propose it is, then?'

'The trickle-down effect we observe when it comes to CEOs is in terms of expectation setting. When the CEOs of private companies earn tens of millions a year, it sets a precedent. It means that the heads of other organizations – like non-profits, charities, and universities - can command compensation of a million or more without looking greedy. In fact, they come off looking humble, frugal, even self-sacrificing in comparison. "Sure, I make over a million a year while asking low-income families to donate to starving children. But that's only a fraction of what I could receive if I worked in the for-profit sector!"'

Hugh looked at Joseph, desperate for him to stop this train wreck. But he seemed to be waiting for Lila to dig herself into a hole. Hugh knew Lila better than that. That woman could talk and talk and talk. She'd

198

wear you down with words, like one of those stones eroded by a drop of water over centuries, until you agreed to whatever she said. Not necessarily agreed with, mind you, but agreed to whatever she said, just so she would leave.

After all, that's how Hugh had agreed to include the word 'beneficial' in the AutoAutomator contract.

'A so-called non-profit can make hundreds of thousands in profit a year and still be classed as a non-profit,' Lila continued to rail. 'A classification which comes with all sorts of tax perks, under one condition. That they funnel the profits into the pockets of their CEOs and other top execs. As long as the profits are transformed into a "salary", the organization can report them as an expense. The money charities receive comes predominantly from some of the country's poorest people, and from government grants – ultimately, from the taxpayer – again, largely sourced from the middle and lower income brackets.'

'You're not genuinely suggesting pensioners and blue collar workers make more charitable donations than the complainants, are you?' Joseph scoffed. 'Mr. Jefferson here is the chair of a tremendously influential organization, the Parker and Melania Jefferson Foundation. Mr. Richardson is a well-known patron of the arts. Ms. Frost is the organizer of the Annual Gala for Feline Dandruff Awareness...'

'It's true that a large chunk of charitable giving comes from the rich as well as the poor,' Lila conceded. 'The richest have the most to spare – and the most to gain in terms of reputation. But the poorest probably have the greatest empathy.'

'That's a rather *uncharitable* interpretation,' Joseph quipped.

'Not at all. Wealth and empathy have been shown to be inversely correlated. Regardless, the amount a CEO is paid also affects how much other high-level executives in a company are paid. Where a CEO earns $20 million a year, it seems reasonable for second-tier execs to get $10 million, and for third-tier management to each be paid a million or more.'

'And there we have it!' Joseph triumphed. 'The trickle down effect!'

'But it never trickles all the way down. The more money that goes to the top, the less that is available for everyone else. At the bottom of the pyramid, these companies still rely on hundreds or thousands of employees making minimum wage, or, through offshoring, less than minimum wage.'

Hugh looked at his watch. Surely the judge would grant them another recess soon. Hugh was desperate for a coffee, even if it was from one of those hideous paper cups – and even more desperate to see Lila step down from the stand.

CHAPTER 19

As Hugh watched the final expert take the stand, something inside him twinged.

The name Joseph had mentioned meant nothing to him. Her qualifications meant less than nothing.

But as Hugh's eyes bored into the woman's rear as she turned to take her seat, an uncomfortable sense of familiarity washed over him.

'Please state your name and occupation for the record.'

'Shawna Fennick, Professor of Economics at CNR University.'

'And how do you know the complainant?' Marshall asked.

'I was retained in connection with Mr. Richardson's divorce settlement hearing.'

Hugh felt sick.

That's where he'd seen her behind before.

Joseph was quick to his feet. 'I have to object to Mr. Richardson's personal life being dragged into this proceedings. His divorce is irrelevant to his performance as CEO.'

Marshall made a quick interjection himself. 'I have here an invoice for Professor Fennick's services. Paid in full by CGM, on the basis that, and I quote, "The satisfactory resolution of Mr. Richardson's divorce is vital to ensure his continued performance as CEO".'

Hugh blistered. The words rolled off Marshall's tongue primarily because he'd been the one to pen them in the first place.

'Your witnesses have spent much of this case testifying as to the importance of personality and personal attributes in the performance of CEO duties. Mr. Richardson's personal life would thus seem highly relevant. Besides, the terms of his divorce are a matter of public record, and are relevant to the nature of Mr. Richardson's current claims.'

'You will need to demonstrate that, but proceed.'

'Professor Fennick, can you describe your area of research please?'

'I study the role of luck in determining wealth. The question is an important one. If wealth comes mainly from luck, then those who earn or possess large sums of money owe a greater debt to society. Perhaps through the form of increased charitable donations, or higher taxation. But, if wealth is a result of hard work and skill, increasing taxation and charitable demands on the wealthy may stymie innovation.'

That's precisely what Hugh had been arguing for years! Perhaps this Fennick woman was still on his side after all.

'What does the research say?'

'There is a general consensus that broad market forces tend to have a much larger influence on a company's fortunes than any individual CEO's decisions.'

Hugh's heart fell.

'And how do you define "luck", Professor?'

'A complex web of interwoven forces are at play. But in general, we refer to them as "luck" because the complexity is so great, no individual can compute all the possibilities. Not even a computer program can – yet.'

Hope filled Hugh's heart once more. Listening to this woman's testimony was like being on a roller coaster. Hugh hoped his lunch would stay down.

'Professor, the experts for the plaintiffs have used terms like "talent". How is "luck" any more concrete? Isn't it the case that, within any environment, a more talented team will do better than a less talented one?'

'It's an appealing idea in principle. But time and time again, we see examples of sheer luck impacting the measures commonly described as "performance". Such as stock price. Take the example of Hootblock, the social media giant which had its initial public offering a few years ago. The day Hootblock went public, stocks in a similarly named tiny company, Hotblock, which manufactures pizza oven stones, went through the roof. As did stocks in Hardings Bank Corporation, and Herbert Bearing Holdings, an even tinier company dealing in ball bearings. The only similarities between these companies was their similar stock tickers. HBC and HBH as opposed to HBK. The CEOs of Hotblock, Hardings Bank and Herbert Bearings had done nothing to warrant a hike in stock price. And yet all three shot up overnight. Doubling – even tripling in the case of Herbert Bearings.'

'But these are short-lived anomalies, exceptions?'

'True. But what happened when investors realized Hotblock, or HBC or HBH wasn't Hootblock? They dumped their shares, selling them off at a fraction of what they'd paid for them. The stock price of Herbert Bearings in particular plummeted. In fact, it still hasn't recovered. A long-term impact, again resulting from luck. Nothing to do with any decision by the CEO of Herbert Bearings.'

'So you acknowledge the role of "bad luck" too?'

'Bad luck plays a big role in understanding why CEOs are fired.'

Tell me about it, Hugh thought.

'It's not unusual for a CEO to lose their job when a company is going through a period of poor performance based on factors beyond the leadership's control. CEOs are more likely to lose their jobs when their industry is in a slump, or when the market as a whole is in a recession. When things are going bad, sacrificing the CEO can help appease the masses.'

'That doesn't sound fair.' Marshall pouted. For a moment, Hugh hoped he might actually be on his side too, deep down.

'Of course it isn't. But neither are the huge layoffs that happen to the rank-and-file employees during tough times. Or the huge layoffs that occur when a CEO does indeed steer the business poorly. And in spite of the fact that CEOs are more likely to be fired when luck isn't going their way, they are still much less likely to be fired due to bad luck than they are to be rewarded for good luck.'

'Surely CEOs object to this characterization of their performance as down to luck?'

'Actually, the best-performing CEO according to Hardly Business Review admitted in an interview five years ago that luck was the single most important factor in his achievement of that ranking. Additionally, the Review found that the influence of each CEO in the ranking accounted for at most 22%, but often, as low as 2% of a company's performance.'

'So you're saying a CEO might be accountable for as much as 22% of a company's profits?'

'Not at all. That figure refers to the difference between one company and another in the same industry. For instance, take two oil companies: one might make a 7% return, the other, 5%. That's a difference of 2% in profit. And an influential CEO might be responsible for 22% of that difference.'

'I'm not good with numbers,' Marshall grinned. More pandering. Marshall could tot up figures in his head like nobody's business. 'Can you help me out here?'

'That would be 0.0044%' Professor Fennick said.

'That doesn't sound like much,' Marshall frowned.

'Well, consider the less influential CEO. One responsible for just 2% of this 2% difference. That's only 0.0004%.'

'Put that into terms I can understand.'

Hugh scowled in his seat. To be honest, he couldn't follow the figures. He hadn't followed them the first time he'd heard this spiel from the professor either, but he knew damn well Marshall could. And equally well that they weren't going to make him look good.

'How much would that be if, for example, the company made a million dollars?'

'If Company A made a million dollars, and Company B outperformed them by 2%, that would mean an additional $20,000 in profit.'

'That's not to be sneezed at.'

'No. But the CEO would only be directly responsible for somewhere between $400 and $4,400 of this gain. And remember – a CEO's influence isn't always positive. Sometimes, it represents a loss!'

'So Professor Fennick, is this range of 2 to 22% reported in the media agreed upon by scholars?'

'Academic studies have been more conservative, estimating that CEOs are responsible only for 4 to 5% of a company's performance.'

'I suppose most CEOs aren't too happy about this?' Marshall smiled.

'On the contrary – most CEOs are only too happy to acknowledge the influence of luck. When things are going badly!'

'What do you mean?'

'Annual reports tend to attribute a company's good performance to the skill of the CEO. But poor performance is attributed to the general economic climate. What we might call luck.'

'Is there any hard evidence to demonstrate the influence of luck on how a CEO's performance is perceived?'

'Absolutely. A recent study found that when luck favored a particular CEO's company or industry, their pay was likely to increase by 25%. They were rewarded for something they had very little or even no hand in.'

'Thank you, professor. I believe we've established the fundamentals of your field. Now, can you elaborate on why your services were engaged by Mr. Richardson?'

Heat rose in Hugh's body. Marshall knew damn well why he'd hired that Fennick woman! After all, Marshall had been the one to select her, to arrange her testimony, to charge her fee to the company!

'I was employed by Mr. Richardson's legal team to analyze and provide an estimate of the degree to which his financial success had been a product of his own effort, and how much was a product of external forces. Luck, or being "in the right place at the right time", so to speak.'

'In your analysis, what factors did you describe as "luck"?'

'Anything outside of Mr. Richardson's control. Such as other company's technology. The expertise of his deputies. Global oil and commodity prices which affect CGM's subsidiaries, and so on.'

'And what was your conclusion?'

'My team of researchers and I arrived at the conclusion that Mr. Richardson was responsible for somewhere in the realm of 5-10% of his corporate success.'

'How did Mr. Richardson take this news?' Marshall asked.

Hugh wanted to smack the man across the face. Marshall knew exactly how Hugh had reacted! He'd been sitting right next to him!'

'I had the impression he was thrilled,' Professor Fennick sniffed.

'Calls for speculation!' Joseph almost tripped over his shoelaces as he rose from the desk.

'I'll rephrase. If your analysis showed Mr. Richardson was only responsible for 10% or less of his success, why were you asked to testify on his behalf?'

'Mr. Richardson's wife – ex-wife, Ms. Bambi Hewlitt-Richardson – was suing Mr. Richardson for half his assets. Under the laws of Mr. and Mrs. Richardson's home state, active and passive income are treated differently in the event of divorce. Where a spouse owns an asset prior to marriage – as Mr. Richardson did with the bulk of his CGM shares, which he received as a sign-on bonus to the company – any increase on these assets is not subject to division because of passive appreciation.'

'What is passive appreciation?'

'Where an asset – such as your bank balance, home, or in Mr. Richardson's case, the share price of his stocks – increases in value due to factors outside of your control. Say you owned a block of land before getting married, valued at $100,000. If you divorce ten years later, without having done anything to the land, it might have appreciated in value, say to $200,000. This $100,000 increase would be considered passive appreciation, since you didn't take an active role in causing it. And it would not be subject to division in the event of divorce. You would thus get to keep the block of land. Had you taken an active role – putting up better fencing, connecting sewerage and electricity, paving the road to the land – even putting up a house or other building-'

'Just like in a board game.'

'Yes, just like in a board game. Well, that would be considered active appreciation. Any active appreciation during the term of the marriage would be subject to division. Just like other monies earned during that relationship, such as salary. Anything that increases in value due to the efforts, skills, or funding of the spouse may be subject to this rule, and hence, divided in the event of a divorce.'

'Did Ms. Hewlitt-Richardson's lawyers accept your estimation of Mr. Richardson's role in the active appreciation of his stocks at 10%?'

'No. Ms. Hewlitt-Richardson's attorney argued that Mr. Richardson was personally responsible for over 90% of the increase in his stock holdings of the company.'

'Your honor, this is hearsay!'

'Ms. Hewlitt-Richardson's attorney's arguments are a matter of public record. Would you prefer I quote from the case?'

Marshall picked up a piece of paper – magically, he always seemed to have the right one exactly to hand – and read aloud. 'I contend that Mr. Richardson was personally responsible for over 90% of the increase in his stock holdings of the company.'

'Very well, you may proceed.'

'Professor, that must have been a pretty interesting case! Mr. Richardson arguing that he was the beneficiary of dumb luck, while his ex-wife argued that he was a brilliant man responsible for more than 90% of the increase in his company's valuation!'

'Indeed. But there was very little evidence to show Mr. Richardson was responsible for anywhere near that figure. The argument of Ms. Hewlitt-Richardson's legal team was that he was almost single-handedly responsible for the company's success. And that all fifteen thousand other employees collectively contributed just 10% of the company's increase in stock price.'

'Professor, you were called upon to analyze the evidence presented by Ms. Hewlitt-Richardson's legal team. What evidence did they present?'

'Her lawyers called around eighty witnesses to testify to Mr. Richardson's role in key meetings and decisions.'

'Were any of the plaintiffs present called? Mr. Park, Mr. Jefferson, Ms. Frost, Mr. Harding?'

'Yes.'

'And why did they decide to testify?'

'Objection!' Joseph shouted, spittle flying across the room 'Calls for speculation!'

Hugh didn't need to hear the answer, and he was sure nobody else in the courtroom did either. They already knew.

They had to testify, because they had to defend the board's decision to pay him his salary all those years.

'Professor Fennick, what evidence did you use to arrive at your conclusion?'

'Aside from our comparisons of Mr. Richardson to other CEOs, and of his company to other similar companies, we also looked at what happened when the variables we defined as external forces – or "luck" - were not going his way.'

'How were you able to do that?'

'At one point, Mr. Richardson experienced a 50% drop in his fortune as a result of falling stock prices. This was almost entirely attributable to a fall in oil prices which affected several of CGM's major subsidiaries. We were able to determine that, more than any other factor, the fortunes of CGM were tied to the fortunes of the industry, and the market as a whole. Rather than to any changes in strategy Mr. Richardson announced, or decisions he made.'

'And how did the court rule?'

Hugh didn't need to hear the answer to this question, either. It had been his biggest victory, etched into his mind forever.

'Ultimately, the judge sided with Mr. Richardson. That is to say, he agreed that Mr. Richardson was only responsible for less than 10% of his company's increase in stock value.'

'Professor, could you read the summary of your analysis the presiding judge made?'

'It is clear from Professor Fennick's analysis that Mr. Richardson has been the beneficiary of a set of particularly favorable conditions during his tenure as CEO. The corporate ship of CGM, has benefited from a rising tide, smooth seas, the wind in its sails, and the expertise of its sailors. Yet when asked under oath about key facts and important decisions, Mr. Richardson testified that he couldn't remember them. He has argued that he doesn't know much about the company's core business, and that he did not attend critical meetings. Thus, I find there is little to indicate that Mr. Richardson has been more than a passenger on this ship, rather than playing an active role as captain.'

Hugh heard none of Joseph's cross-examination, his babbling and bobbing as if he were underwater.

The ship had already sunk.

CHAPTER 20

'Ladies and gentlemen, this is a case about taking responsibility. About a company – AutoAutomator – taking responsibility for the pain and suffering it has caused my clients.

When Mr. Richardson and the other members of this class action met Kira, an AutoAutomator salesperson, they were promised the best decision of their lives. Software that would not only increase profits, but boost their careers.

Instead, this malicious software took their careers away.

Throughout this case, we've heard a lot of criticism of my clients. That they earn too much. Are too insular. Won't accept new ideas.

But what has the AutoAutomator replaced these CEOs with?

More old white men.

Some might argue that it doesn't really matter what face the company has when that face is a computer-generated amalgamation of CEO-like faces.

But what of the decisions these AutoCEOs have made since their introduction?

It's the status quo.

AutoCEOs are trained on these former CEOs' decisions.

Their prejudices. Their biases.

In short, their intellectual property.

Learning from their predecessors, AutoCEOs have continued to discriminate.

Continued to erode the rights of workers.

Continued to avoid social, environmental, and financial responsibility for the damage caused by the companies they run.

Mr. Marshall may argue that the amount these human CEOs were paid was obscene. Unwarranted. Damaging to social cohesion, even.

Ladies and gentlemen, I agree.

Nobody deserves to earn in a year what would take their employees fifty lifetimes to earn.

But recall that all-important word in the AutoAutomator contract.

Beneficial.

The fact that an AutoCEO costs less is not sufficient cause to automate my clients' jobs away, according to the contract my clients had with AutoAutomator.

AutoAutomator must also demonstrate that the tasks of a CEO can be more beneficially performed via automation – something they have not done, and indeed, will never be able to do.

Technology is not neutral. The AutoAutomator software, by training its automatically generated CEOs solely on data sourced from past, human CEOs, is inherently flawed. AutoCEOs cannot be better than a human CEO because they are designed to emulate them.

Data is powerful. Big data even more so.

But with increased power comes increased danger.

Diversity is not about ticking boxes, or ensuring a rainbow of skin colors and hairstyles in a corporate brochure. Companies can still lack meaningful representation if they only hire those from the same sorts of wealthy, well-connected backgrounds to the top jobs. Those who attended the same business schools, who have been taught to think in the same way.

In some countries, corporate boards must consist of at least 50% workers.'

Joseph, Hugh was certain, had lost his mind.

'This not only brings about much-needed socioeconomic diversity, ensuring the board isn't 'out-of-touch' with their customers, but also helps to motivate workers and make them feel as if they are part of something bigger. More importantly, it helps CEOs to become more respectful of their workers.

With greater diversity comes a better mix of leadership skills, a wider pool of talent, and a better understanding of consumer groups.

Ladies and gentlemen, there is a better way. A more beneficial way to run companies. A way which, almost certainly, involves leaning even more heavily on computers to make decisions.

But first, we have to train them correctly. Not based upon the biases and mistakes of the past. But on the way we want to see our future.'

A strange feeling flooded Hugh as Joseph sat back down next to him.

The feeling that they might actually win.

But also that he wasn't sure he wanted his old job back.

'Ladies and gentlemen,' Marshall began. 'My learned colleague has rightly characterized this case as concerning responsibility. We have heard how Mr. Richardson and the rest of his class have consistently denied responsibility for any of their or their company's failings, while demanding obscene levels of pay.

You've heard Ms. Dryser describe these obscene amounts as "compensation". A euphemism for private jets and tropical villas and multi-million-dollar bonuses.

According to the dictionary, "compensation" refers to the act of compensating someone for a loss, damage, or injury, or for a service, via an appropriate benefit. Consider that word: an *appropriate* reward.

In the field of psychology, "compensation" refers to an individual's attempts to make whole a real or imagined deficit.

Ladies and gentlemen, I believe that the pay the plaintiffs have been commanding for the duration of their careers has been closer to this second, specialized definition of compensation. That is, rather than being rewarded appropriately for the benefit they have delivered to their respective companies, these gentlemen have been compensated for largely imagined contributions.

Is it not then appropriate that they be replaced by imaginary CEOs?

We have heard Mr. Rich liken the CEOs gathered here to surgeons, lawyers, and professional athletes. But with even the slightest application of scrutiny, Mr. Rich's analogy crumbles.

A surgeon without an assistant can still perform surgery. Not as effectively, yet in an emergency, they can certainly still do so. A lawyer without a paralegal can still bring a case to court.'

Hugh imagined he saw Marshall shoot a pointed look at Joseph. As if he knew what a run-down hovel of an office he had.

'And an athlete without a coach or a nutritionist or trainer can still play football or tennis or golf. Maybe not at the top of their game, but still, to an exceptionally high standard.'

Marshall paused. One of those big pauses he took that used to fill Hugh with such glee, as he watched the anxious faces across the other side of the court.

'Yet, the inverse is not true. You don't see a sports masseuse subbing in for a pro-league athlete. A paralegal doesn't step in to try a case in the qualified lawyer's absence. A surgical assistant is not only legally prohibited from carrying out operations, but almost certainly does not possess the skills and training to do so even in an emergency – in fact, medical associations recommend waiting for professional help. You won't find the lighting guy and manager replacing the singer and guitarist everyone has come to see. They'd be run off the stage!

Is this what we see happen when a CEO is replaced? No!

Employees – the majority of whom have never seen or even heard the name of their CEO – don't notice.

Stockholders don't notice.

And as we have seen in this court, even the board and the CEOs themselves don't notice. There is no one clamoring in the factories or office buildings or in the streets to bring back these former CEOs.

What happens when you take the team away from a CEO, though?

You take away the employees of CGM's oil drilling subsidiaries, and guess what? No oil is drilled.

You stand down the foreign workers who produce ToyStar's GI John dolls and no dolls are produced.

The CEOs who are the complainants in this case have been unable to demonstrate that they have an effect on their companies commensurate with the salaries they receive. And really, should we be surprised? They are individuals after all – though we might be forgiven for forgetting that, given that they earn hundreds, or thousands of times what their other employees do.

In fact, as we have heard from both Mr. Rich and Ms. Owen, the main way in which a CEO influences a company is via their pay packages. The bigger the gap between the CEO's pay and the pay of workers, the less motivated workers tend to be, and the worse the company's performance as a result.

You've heard Professor Colbert's testimony that the ratio of CEO to worker pay is arbitrary, and not worth questioning. My learned colleague, in asking you to focus on the "beneficial" clause in the contract, is essentially doing the same.

It is easy to dismiss something as arbitrary when it doesn't apply to you. The typical pay ratio of a university president to a professor is around 4:1. Some internationally renowned scholars – generally in the fields of medicine, and unsurprisingly, business – even out-earn their presidents.

But the ratios we've heard in this case are far beyond those affecting Professor Colbert's career. We're talking not about 4 to 1, but 400 to 1, or even 4,000 to 1. While it might take Professor Colbert four years to earn as much as the president of the University of Hardville, a worker at Mr. Richardson's company would take five lifetimes of non-stop cradle-to-grave work to earn as much as he does in a single year.

And even if a worker at one of Ms. Frost's factories spent their whole life making dolls, as did her daughter, and then her daughter's daughter, for sixty generations, that worker and the sixty generations under her would still not have earned as much as Ms. Frost did last year. To these workers, the perverse ratios of CEO to worker pay these gentlemen would have us endorse are far from arbitrary.

As Ms. Owen has testified, relative inequality is important. Big corporations don't simply fail to pay their workers fairly. Low-paid workers additionally suffer because big corporations refuse to pay their fair share of tax, use their vast wealth to lobby for even lower taxes, and fail to pay their workers enough to fund their own insurance, social security, or retirement funds. Those who fall on hard times have to rely on the kindness of charities, who are often either beholden to corporations for donations, or are themselves corporations, with CEOs earning millions.

And relative poverty leads to absolute poverty. CEO pay has grown at roughly double the rate of the stock market itself. Because the gap is widening so much, eventually those at the top will control so much of the money that what little those down the bottom have will be worthless.

We have heard over and over references to the board. To shareholders. And occasionally, to workers and customers. But you'll notice that the very reason a CEO to worker ratio is possible to calculate is because the CEO is never classified as a worker. A worker is defined as "a person or thing that works". An executive on the other hand, is simply a person – or in the case of the AutoCEO, a program, "vested with authority in an organization".

Ladies and gentlemen, we have heard that the fund managers, in charge of voting in their members' best interests, have been asleep at the wheel for years, when it comes to voting down exorbitant compensation packages. While the views of the public are clear, these mutual and pension funds, which ostensibly have the ability to hold CEOs to task, have been complicit in permitting CEOs to get away with receiving excessive payments for far too long.

Today, you have an opportunity to make your voices heard. To vote, not in a non-binding charade the board will ignore, but to send a powerful message not only to the overpaid CEOs bringing this suit against a struggling start-up, but to every other CEO in the world.'

As Hugh sat on the courthouse steps, waiting for the verdict, he came to his own conclusion.

He was going to write his own book.

By himself this time, without outsourcing or automating a single word.

But first, he was going to live a life worth writing about.

ABOUT THE AUTHOR

Sarah Neofield

Sarah Neofield is a writer, linguist and
traveller currently studying mathematics
and programming.

AutoCEO is her third novel, following
Number Eight Crispy Chicken and
Propaganda Wars.

Find out more at
www.sarahneofield.com

ACKNOWLEDGEMENTS

An enormous thanks as always to Simon N. for the blue screen of death inspired cover design, and everything else you do for me, and to Simon P. for the font input!

While Hugh and his friends, and their companies, are of course figments of my imagination, the facts and figures of the case built in *AutoCEO* are based on real life. You can find a list of references and further reading on my website, sarahneofield.com/resources

OTHER BOOKS BY THIS AUTHOR

Number Eight Crispy Chicken

The immigration minister has been detained.
Minister for Asylum Deterrence and Foreign Investment, Peter Ruddick, is en route to the remote Pulcherrima Island, the site of his latest privately-run, fast food chain-inspired detention centre. But chaos ensues when Peter misses his connecting flight and finds himself confined to the visa-free zone of the Turgrael airport, without a business lounge in sight.

Stranded in a foreign territory with nothing but McKing's Crispy Chicken burgers to eat and nobody but a bleeding heart liberal, his seat-mate Jeremy Bernard for company, Peter's misunderstandings of Turgistani language and culture result in his arrest on suspicion of terrorism, perversion, and espionage. Peter has always had the power to get away with just about anything, but how will he sweet talk his way out of this one? What if he winds up - like those in his centres - indefinitely detained?

Propaganda Wars

The most powerful messages are the ones you don't see.

After decades of knowing nothing of the Souwest other than her collection of McKing's wrappers that occasionally blew over the wall, Noreastern Ministry propagandist Adria crosses the border on a professional exchange to one of the Souwest's top advertising companies.

And that means her ad-exec cousin, Wesley, is coming to the Noreast - not to spread freedom, but french fries and fizzy cola.

It's only for a week, but will Adria finally taste the freedom she long dreamed of just beyond the wall?

And why does Wesley feel freer than he did back in the land of the free?

Grab your copy of Propaganda Wars today and join the fight!

'Neofield's prose is flawless, with deep multi dimensional characters that capture your attention from the jump... Propaganda Wars is a war you'll be excited to enlist to fight in.' - Wesley Parker, author of Coffee and Condolences, and Headphones and Heartaches.

Praise for Sarah Neofield's debut novel, Number Eight Crispy Chicken:
'...thought provoking entertainment... five stars' - Whispering Stories, www.whisperingstories.com

www.ingramcontent.com/pod-product-compliance
Lightning Source LLC
Chambersburg PA
CBHW031949170626
46807CB00006B/2416